DÚNMHARÚ
The Favor

DON FOXE

CABALLUS
PRESS™

Copyright © 2018 don foxe

This is a work of fiction. Names, characters, businesses, places, events and incidents are either the products of the author's imagination or used in a fictitious manner. Any resemblance to actual persons, living or dead, or actual events is purely coincidental.

Written by Don Foxe. donfoxe.com

Produced by Caballus Press, USA Division
www.caballuspress.com

Stock images are used for illustrative purposes only.
Some stock imagery from Pixabay.com, Unsplach.com, and Stock-Adobe.com

ISBN: 978-1-7321036-2-7
ISBN: 978-1-7321036-3-4 (e)

Library of Congress Control Number: (TBA)

Acknowledgments

My love and appreciation to Sarah for continuing to support my late-night hours squirreled away in my office. Your input on everything I write helps me realize how much I cannot do without you. Outside of writing, I simply cannot do without you.

Thanks to G.L. Pease, creator of wondrous tobacco blends, and Cornell and Diehl of Morganton, North Carolina, the company that manufactures the final products for allowing me to use their names and brands.

www.glpease.com   www.cornellanddiehl.com

Word-up to Nancy Thurmond for editing. In those places you find the grammar questionable, those are my decisions to add *style* over substance. She shakes her head, but allows me artistic license.

Author's back cover photograph courtesy of *Abri Kruger Photography*, South Africa.

DÚNMHARÚ

THE SEVEN GATES
THE FAVOR

SPACE FLEET SAGAS

CONTACT AND CONFLICT
CONFRONTATION
CONFLUENCE
CONNEXIONS

SPACE FLEET SAGAS
A Collection of Adventures.

POETRY

SEASONS OF HENKA SURU w/ Melissa Dolber Grappone
HAIKU SEISHIN w/ Melissa Dolber Grappone
PARANORMAL POETRY: A Chapbook Of Poems By Ghosts Of The South Carolina Lowcountry.

donfoxe.com

Pandaemonium

Their blood, mixed with his sweat, made it difficult to focus. The unpleasant mélange seared his eyes. Violently shaking his head to fling off the oily beads helped for a second, but no longer. His brown hair, stained dark auburn, funneled the fluids back onto his forehead to flow over his brow and again blur his vision.

"One-hundred-yards," Oberon called. His King called the distance from a step to his left and two steps back. The Lord of the Seelie parried sword strokes with his battle lance. The weapon forged by the Fairy Blade-smith, Fearghas. The double-edged leaf-shaped tip could pierce the armor of an attacker. Beneath the tip, one side held a sharpened hook and the other a square-faced hammer. Oberon could rip a shield aside, or pound a helmet into the skull of the unlucky opponent within range of the weapon's six-foot reach.

Fearghas attached the business end to a shaft carved of bone from a sea serpent. The bone shaft kept the cold steel of the blade, hook, and hammer from burning the Fae. Leather wrapping and a vamplate of the same bone allowed the King to wield the long lance without it slipping from his grasp.

Sionnach fought with two swords. His shaska and a short broadsword of obsidian plucked from the hand of a dead dullahan. He always considered tales of an evil headless Fae killer as boogeyman stories. Confronted by a real headless-horseman (sans horse), he sliced the miscreant from groin to belly.

The two, King and King's Claidheamh, nearly reached the exit portal before the troop of UnSeelie reached them. Nearly. The exit gate located halfway up a hillside, one-hundred-fifty-yards above the roadway.

Not a bucolic slope of grass and flowers. A hill of crumbling stones, deep fissures, and sharp outcroppings. It would be a difficult climb without one-hundred hybrid experiments and outcasts from suspicious breedings attempting to slaughter you. At least the craggy bank kept their opponents from flanking the pair as they retreated.

No more than six of the UnSeelie could confront the two inter-lopers at once. Helpful, but as Oberon or Sionnach felled an at-tacker, another quickly took their place. The game became attri-tion against exhaustion. The two Fae boasted incredible stamina, but not without limits. Fighting a hoard of dark fairies while climbing a steep slope backwards would test those limits.

"Seventy-five," Oberon called, his hammer driving a dark elf's head deeply into its chest. Pointed ears now looked like tiny wings on its shoulders.

A bone-thin hag took the elf's place. She whirled a chain of sil-ver with compact spikes forged to the links. Her visage reminded Sionnach why they found themselves in the midst of a battle where death would not be the worst possible ending.

"Ugly creatures, dey was," the dwarf mayor told them.

Oberon and Sionnach sat in the hut of the woman designated Mayor of the village. The village nestled between a fresh-water lake and a cavern with a dimensional gate entrance. The dwarves, a gregarious and friendly race, welcomed visitors to their world.

"Dey came through the gate with big black animals what had big ears and extended snouts." The woman used her hands to add emphasis to her words. "Big teeth. Four-legged. Tails like whips. Howled as dey rushed around."

The Mayor whipped her own hand through the air. "The hags used shiny metal chains with teeth. Cut right way through clothes and ripped skin from bone."

She took a break to down a sizable mug of the local brew. The two Fae visitors received tankards in welcome, once they proved to be no danger. Both imbibed many a strong concoction across dimensions and galaxies. This brew blew them away in pure alco-holic kick. Sionnach wondered if the dwarf's story might be a delusion caused by the drink.

"We're not a warrior race, but we know how to defend our home," the Mayor told them. "Not every visitor coming though the gate is as nice as you fine gentlemen. The townsfolk grabbed spears and tools to fight off the hags and beasts. Took some doing, but we drove 'em down to the lake and showed 'em the way to the nearest exit. I went with my best people to keep trail for six days to make sure dey didn't try to turn back. Those nasty bitches caused us two-weeks of work."

"Do you have any idea where they came from, or where they went?" Oberon asked. For two millennia the Seelie sovereign followed rumors of dark beings with characteristics similar to the Folk. Canards of a Black Queen building a world of terrible creatures, and hiring the worse mercenaries to support her rule. Hearsay of Pandaemonium.

"I followed 'em for two gates, Plane-travel is something we do. Trade a fair bit among other worlds," she said as explanation why following them did not seem foolhardy. "Dey gots all befuddled before dey exited the second way station. I stayed hid, couldn't understand their jibber, but think maybe dey were afraid dey was going to be punished for being showed off our world. Gave me the willy-gees," she said, a shiver to emphasize the truth of her story. "I came back. Took an entire star-rise to star-down to find a different exit. At least it took us to a place I'd seen before. Got home slick."

"Fifty," Oberon said. His tone labored. Stationed behind Sionnach, he kept watch on the portal and the hill above. A number of the troop, realizing they could not launch an attack in mass, rode off on their animals. They would ride hard to circle the wide mound, scale it from the backside, and attack from over the top.

Sionnach kept the King back by explaining the importance of the position. He kept the King back to better protect him.

The dwarf mayor led them to the last gated location she saw the hags and hounds. A black opal, cut and polished so the myriad of colors within the gemstone sparkled, given as payment for her information and assistance. She told them the location of the second local exit portal and subsequent gates she used to plane-travel home.

Oberon was no coward, but as the Lord and Monarch of Tir na Nog, he could not be allowed to plane-travel unprotected. Sionnach Catharnagh, his son, became his personal guard - his Claidheamh - following decades of training. Training designed by, often instructed by, and always directed by the Maerrighan. The Battle Raven, Goddess of Warriors, Council to the King, and the most complex being to ever exist in any of the nine dimensions. It became the son's duty to protect the King; sometimes from himself.

"When we reach the entry, remain in the passage," he instructed. The King gave orders except when his safety became an issue. Sionnach gave the orders then. "I will scout the area. We need to know where the nearest exit is located before you step onto an uncharted world."

"I know the drill," Oberon replied. "I set up my little camp and the king waits with his thumbs up his royal arse until you beckon."

"It's kept us alive before. You are immortal, not invulnerable."

"While you are invulnerable, but not immortal."

They both smiled at the oft-repeated phrases.

He used his ring and mother's incantation to release a magical barrier warding the portal. Odd, but not the first time. Magic and science were evenly spread throughout the universe as a whole. Some dimensions more driven by forms of sorcery, and others enhanced by technology. The vast majority of gates encountered were not guarded. He left the ward down, in case Oberon had no other choice but to leave the passage.

Oberon rested and ate two light meals before Sionnach returned from exploring.

"It isn't the strangest or ugliest world we have visited," his son informed him. "I met a couple of sentients. Nasty attitudes, but no one tried to kill me. I saw a few wild beasts. They had traits like Fae animals, and some I thought to be extinct. More importantly I saw a castle made entirely of black stone. It looked exactly like your palace in Ireland."

"We found her," the King said. The words said low, with little breath behind them. "After untold centuries, we have located Pandaemonium. The creatures ignored you?"

"Yes."

"You did not get too near the black castle?"

"No."

"You found an exit gate?"

"Was told about it by a fanged fairy and confirmed it. Less than a ten-minute fast walk from this entrance."

"I want to see everything for myself," Oberon said. He gathered his kit, lifted his lance, and the two walked into hell.

A ten-foot-tall curly haired troll with a bulbous red nose forced its way through the smaller soldiers queued on the hillside below those involved in fighting. It arrived after the mounted mix of Un-Seelie. From higher on the hill, more creatures could be seen converging on the location. Riders, and beings two-legged, four-and-more-legged, and something serpentine slithering across the rocky landscape.

The troll roared unintelligible curses, backhanding smaller dark Fae aside as he advanced. He, not it or she, if a thick, wrinkled penis hanging below a dirty kilt meant the same here as on Earth. A massive cudgel in hand to deliver mayhem.

Looking up at the troll's hideous face, Sionnach spied something more frightful.

"Oberon, look!"

A flock of four-legged, winged creatures flew from the direction of the Black Castle. Distant, but near enough to see the beasts were hairless with reddish skin. Bodies akin to a horse or bull, but heads shaped like alligators. Two dozen of them, and each held a rider.

"The Black Queen," Oberon said.

At the front of the flight, a figure in black rode the largest of the steeds. Dark hair streaming, posture perfect as she sat between wings acting as oars, speeding rider and beast powerfully across the bruised-colored sky.

The troll reclaimed their immediate attention. He brushed three gnarled brownies with short swords aside. His grin made more unattractive by spittle oozing from the corners of his mouth and mucus from a nostril flowing across his upper lip. He placed both hands to his club's shaft and raised it overhead.

"The Queen demands they be captured, not killed!" a tall, skinny elf screamed from the bottom of the shale mound.

"Oops," the troll said. Eyes filled with the glee of murder. Eyes that changed expression as dark pupils expanded. The smug grin transformed into a frown.

The splinters, shards, and loose rock making the hillside difficult to negotiate gave way beneath the giant's feet. When he raised the heavy truncheon, his weight shifted. Big feet skated forward as the rest of him toppled backward. Evil brownies, sprites, elves, and beings of questionable heritage were crushed, tossed, and carried down the slope with the flailing ogre.

Sionnach flung the borrowed obsidian blade. The sharp stone penetrating the chest of the last UnSeelie still on the hill. "Go!" he ordered his sire.

Without an assault to defend against, the two covered the final yards to the exit in seconds. Sionnach slammed his palm against the magic barrier, invoked the ward to fall, and pushed Oberon through. Before his king could regain his balance and turn, the Fae Warrior recalled the ward. It rose between the two.

"The Queen will make short work of this barrier," he said to Oberon. "I will hold them to give you time to escape. When you exit find another gate and keep finding them until you lose anyone following. Get back to Tir na Nog, Oberon. You know Pandaemonium is real. The Folk, and Earth must be warned."

Sionnach turned his back on his king. Sword in right hand, dagger drawn by his left, he took the fight to the enemy.

Chapter 1

The early summer heat which plagued most of the Southeastern United States did not reach the upper slopes of Blood Mountain in the dark early morning hours before the sun rose. A gentle
breeze topped the peak, flowing from the North and across the
Appalachian range. It carried the scent of pine and relief from the
infamous Georgia humidity.

Cale sat on the side of the trail, below the rim of the mountain
top. His back rested against the trunk of a tree uprooted and
thrown to the ground during a storm a quarter-century before.
The serenity of the moment countered by whisking thoughts of
the potential peril he came to face.

"You're the Dúnmharú." The statement made from beside and
behind his right ear.

Had he not been expecting someone to contact him, the utter-
ance might have startled him. He knew a watcher waited nearby.
He felt their presence since arriving and taking a seat.

"I am. You are?" he asked without turning.

His visitor jumped from the log to the ground beside him. Ten-
inches tall with a humanoid body. Cale Kearney possessed enhanced night vision, one of his half-Fae qualities, but colors tended to fade together in the darkness. This being had wild dark hair,
wide dark eyes, a pointed nose, thin lips, and appeared to be some
forest shade of green. He was nude.

"Justice," the diminutive Fae replied. "I'm a dryad, in case you
did not know."

"I thought you were," Cale answered. "I have never seen a
male dryad."

"And yet, here I am," the little man said, hands on hips.
"Someone has to keep the females satisfied. Are you checking to
make sure we're on the job?"

"No. Puck told me Titania ordered the entrances and exits to
the Nunnehi kingdom watched. I doubt any Folk would fail to respond to the Queen's command. You said, 'we.' Are other dryads
nearby?"

"It's my watch until sunrise," Justice replied. "Constance will take my place. There are six of us. The forests for hundreds of miles are ours."

Dryads were a type of nymph. They lived within trees, and preferred oaks. Territories were important to a dryad, and a clan would fight to maintain their dominion. Unless threatened they were, otherwise, affable, but shy. Justice appeared friendly, but not exactly shy.

"No vampire has entered or departed since we began watching," he assured the Council of Four's Enforcer. "We would have called."

"Called?"

Justice jumped atop the log, and disappeared on the far side. He was gone two-minutes. He returned by walking around the up-rooted end of the fallen tree, struggling to carry something about half his size. He dropped it near Cale.

"A cell phone," Cale remarked. "Dryads have phone service?"

"Liberated from a tourist who set it down without considering its value," the Fae said. "This is the third one I have . . ." he hesitated, realizing he spoke to someone in authority, "found. We do not have battery chargers out here."

"If a vampire showed, you would call Titania by phone?"

"I do not have the Queen's number," Justice replied. "I do have Puck's. Why are you here, Assassin, if not to check on our ability to watch a hole in the ground?"

Dúnmharú, a derivative of an ancient Celtic term, could be translated into any descriptive given to someone who kills others. Justice calling him Assassin was not an insult. If he intended to disrespect Kearney, he could have used a number of more toxic titles.

"I'm here to speak with Adahy," Cale answered.

"The leader of the Nunnehi Tribe," Justice exclaimed. "The Nunnehi despise humans. While you are Dúnmharú, you are also part-human."

"And Half-Fae," Cale said.

"The Nunnehi Fae no longer have anything to do with the rest of us. They are not Folk. Half-Fae and half-human makes you twice as likely to be killed," the dryad said. "Why do you think Adahy would speak with you?"

Cale pulled his backpack onto his lap. He opened the top flap, pushing the overly curious nymph back as the wee Fae attempted to peek inside. He pulled out a carved pipe with a twelve-inch stem. Next came a four-ounce Mason jar, the type with a metal spring bar to seal the contents against air.

"Tobacco," Justice said. His voice breathy as he stared longingly at the glass container. "Good stuff?"

"Haddo's Delight by G.L. Pease," Cale answered. "Several Virginia tobaccos with a generous amount of long-cut perique. Unflavored Green River black Cavendish and a little air-cured white burley ribbon. They add a bit of extra strength."

He flipped the thin metal bar, unscrewed the zinc lid, and pulled off the sealed cap. An aroma of cocoa and dried fruit waifed from the open jar.

Justice had wings, but instead of hovering he lifted high onto his tip-toes to catch the scent of the fresh tobacco. He almost levitated.

"It's wonderful," he said. "The only tobacco we ever get is from cigarette butts."

"The flavor is like figs and raisins," Cale told him. "Blended in Morganton, North Carolina by Cornell and Diehl. The Virginias in the blend are flue-cured, and the cavendish toasted. Air-cured and ribbon-cut for a perfect tobacco to be enjoyed in a pipe."

Cale removed a strong pinch of the leaf and held it out for Justice.

The dryad reached, then froze. His extended hands began to quiver. His pupils, already enlarged for the darkness, grew wider. He was torn by anticipation and fear.

"You owe me nothing in return," Cale said, easing the fairy's fear of being forced into some horrible repayment. "Consider it a bonus for keeping watch."

He wanted so *very* much to snatch the tobacco and run, but the little man controlled himself. He took it from Cale, pulled it close to his chest and breathed the aroma deep into his soul. There would be no thanks. Folk do not say thanks. And it's rude to expect any.

"You think Haddo's Delight will make Adahy talk?" Justice asked.

"I think he will recognize an invitation," Cale answered. "It is up to Adahy if he wants to talk. Right, Adahy?"

Cale did not startle when Justice tried to sneak up on him, but Justice became flustered when the Nunnehi spirit warrior materialized at Cale's feet. Discomposed by Adahy's arrival, and equally frightened spying on the Nunnehi's cave entrance might be considered a killable offense, the dryad melted into the forest and the protection of his beloved trees.

"You take a dangerous risk, Dúnmharú. Our truce ended when Arina and her coterie entered our city," the Fae tribal chief said. "When you fought her and her tribe on this mountain, I kept the Shadow Warriors from interfering. I told the Maerrighan it would be the last token offered the Fae Royals."

Cale began to sprinkle tobacco into the bowl of the pipe. When it reached the top, he packed it with his finger, and sprinkled more. If concerned about the lack of a truce, he hid it well.

"The pipe was made by the Cherokee," he said. He spoke aloud, but not directly to the Nunnehi. "It has a red clay bowl and the stem is hollowed oak. It is not the Sacred Pipe of the Creator, but a close cousin."

Cale ignited a wooden match by flicking his right thumbnail against the head. He held it over the tobacco and softly puffed. He did this four times until the bowl glowed a uniform red. He pulled deeply, held the rich flavor, and let it escape slowly. The smoke created an apparition in the air.

"The sun is rising," he said. "The darkness is moving to the West."

He turned the stem of the pipe and held it up to the Fae. Adahy, dressed in the garb of a Cherokee warrior, accepted. He held the pipe in two hands, and dragged deeply into his lungs. As the first rays of morning passed over the pines and oaks atop the ridge, he blew smoke toward the heavens. He eased down beside Cale, sitting cross-legged with his back sharing the fallen tree trunk.

The spirit Fae handed the peace pipe back to the Dúnmharú.

"That is some damn fine tobacco," he said, causing Cale to hiccup while caught between pulling on the stem and choking at Adahy's description.

"What?" the ancient non-terrestrial asked. "You don't think we stay relevant? We have lived in these mountains for over twenty-five-thousand-years, but we are not stuck in the past. Our city has internet."

"Why did you help Arina bring the Blood Dragons here?" he asked. He returned the pipe.

"Anger. Frustration. Humans are destroying everything beautiful about their world. I believed Arina when she told me of a plan to force humans to turn to non-terrestrials to save them." Adahy puffed the pipe. "Arina has lived in these lands nearly as long as the Nunnehi. She came after the first human tribe, and she respected our territories. I did not know she planned on using the Blood Dragons to attack witches."

Cale accepted the stem, taking short puffs, as Adahy before him. He noticed when Justice returned. The little dryad stood on the log beside Cale's head, eyes closed, nasals flared to take in the aroma.

The half-human, half-Fae twisted to hold the protracted stem away and faced the lip toward the dryad.

The nymph placed both hands around the mouthpiece and drew in deeply. When he released the pipe, he lost his balance, landing on his butt atop the tree trunk. He slapped both hands over his mouth to prevent the smoke from escaping.

Adahy chuckled as the fairy slowly allowed the smoke to escape, finishing with a self-satisfied sigh.

"I cannot turn Arina over to you," the chief said. "I gave her and her tribe members sanctuary. We have broken ties with Oberon and Titania. The Nunnehi no longer recognize the authority of the Council of Four."

Cale tapped the bowl, releasing the remaining tobacco from the chamber into his palm. He handed the pipe to Adahy. With his free hand he removed a plastic bag from a pocket on his combat pants. He placed the warm tobacco in, sealed it, and handed the baggie to Justice.

He lifted the Mason jar, replaced the seal, screwed on the cap, and locked the spring-bar over the top. He handed the glass jar to the spirit warrior.

"These are tokens of respect and come with no expectations," he said. "Whatever may follow, know I hold the Nunnehi, and their leader, in high regard."

Cale stood and held his hand out to take Adahy's forearm, assisting the Fae to his feet. In those few seconds, Cale Kearney allowed his Fae-soul to emerge. When the Nunnehi stood facing the young man, he faced Cahal Kearney, the Dúnmharú.

"Arina lied to the Nunnehi. She used you to broker a deal with mercenaries. She brought those killers to our world to destroy harmony. Her only desire is for vampires to rule this planet, and for her to rule the vampires. I am not asking for you to hand her over. I understand your rules of hospitality, and you cannot break those rules. That you have broken ties with the other Fae is between you and them."

The young man spoke with the wisdom of age. His eyes held those of the Nunnehi warrior-chief.

"I would take care, Adahy. Titania has a long fuse, but if she ignites, the flame which follows shows no mercy. It does not matter if you recognize the Council of Four or my authority. I will offer you a deal. A one-time offer. I will not seek punishment for you aiding Arina to bring murderers to this world. In return, you will not stand against me when I arrest Arina and remove her from your city."

"If I do not accept your offer?"

"I will enter, find, and remove Arina anyway. Any who oppose me, vampire or Fae, will die," Cahal said.

"There are thousands of spirits living in our cities," Adahy responded. "You do not have the Maerrighan here to protect you this time."

"You misunderstood Morgan's appearance on Blood Mountain, Adahy. She did not show up to protect me. She came to save the Nunnehi spirits from me. If she comes back, it will be to carry Nunnehi warrior souls home."

The Dúnmharú's voice did not rise, but carried the weight of conviction.

"You say 'arrest'. You are an executioner."

"Not this day," Cahal said. "Arina knows of others who wish to destroy the harmony between humans, witches, vampire, and Fae. It is already a strained relationship, and does not need much to fail. I would rather stop a war than execute one vampire."

"I cannot take away Arina's status. She has sanctuary. I cannot stop her coterie from attacking you if you attack them. I can offer you hospitality, Dúnmharú. Nunnehi spirit warriors will not raise arms against a guest. Even a guest with the poor manners to attack another guest."

Arina lay in the uncomfortable bed. Another restless day in the Nunnehi city beneath the Appalachians. Without sun or stars, she did not feel the pull for sleep, nor the exultation of rising.

The Fae provided blood from forest animals for her and the four scion with her. Unsubstantial and undesirable, but nutrition until she could escape this hell.

Long fingers pushed the dark hair from her face. She rolled from her side to her back.

A dark figure stood beside her bed. The Nunnehi traveled through their world as spirits or solid and human-appearing. There seemed no rhyme or reason to which form they took.

"Have the Nunnehi shadow-warriors taken to watching women in their beds?" she asked.

"Vampires should be cold and ugly."

The realization of her visitor reflected in her dark eyes.

Chapter 2

"He fucking shot me!"

"Watch your language!" the centaur yelled back. "Did it kill yah?"

"No, but he didn't know it wouldn't," the boy replied. He bounced from foot to foot as he rubbed the center of his chest.

"Puck, did you know the bullet would not kill Cahal?" Skerrit, the Fae huntsman with the torso and head of a bodybuilder atop the body of a stallion, called the question to a short man with red hair, beard, and bushy mustache. A little shorter and he would look like a leprechaun. A lot taller he would be a lumberjack.

"Pretty sure," he answered. "His Fae traits have been coming out since his twelfth birthday. His skin should be tough enough to stop most things."

"Most things?" Cahal asked with a wide-eyed look. His tone a mix of horror and anger. "Aren't Fae vulnerable to iron?"

"Most," Puck agreed.

"Steel is made from iron, and bullets have steel jackets," the boy argued.

"The proper term is cartridge, not bullet," Puck replied. "I'm using brass casings, just in case."

"There you go," Skerrit said. "You were safe all along."

The shot rang out, echoing around the hills and gullies of Rockforest in Tipperary.

"He fucking shot me again!" Cahal yelled. He sat on his arse, rubbing his left quad.

"Language, boy!" Skerrit called. "He *Pucking* shot you. Get it? 'Cause his name is Puck. And he, Puck, shot you."

The red-headed Fae held a hand out to the lad. Once he gripped his forearm, he lifted. At the same time, he swung a fisted right hand at the boy's head.

Cahal blocked the punch, twisted and reversed the hold on his arm, sliding his hand over the Fae's. He pressed down and in, forcing Puck to bend over. His right foot stepped past his opponent and swung back, sweeping the thick-built Royal off his stance and onto his back.

The boy, whose eyes had gone from dark brown to darker tar, released the Fae as he fell. He picked up the revolver, dropped when Puck pretended to help Cahal off the ground. He cocked and fired in one motion, the slug tearing into the hard-packed earth, inches from Puck's left ear.

"Anything else you want to test?" he asked.

"Not today, Nephew. Not today," Puck repeated.

The centaur pranced. Skerrit laughed like a loon.

"We have to find out what you are capable of," the Fae Royal said after rising from the dirt. He reached out, palm up.

Cahal placed the chrome-plated pistol in Puck's hand.

"'Tis the truth," Skerrit said, trotting back to join the two. Neither Cahal nor Puck stood taller than the centaur's withers. "You're a bit odd, Cahal. Part human and part Fae. That's near as rare as Puck lending money."

"Maybe if someone would tell me who my Fae father is, it might be a clue as to what I am," Cahal countered.

"Not our place, and not the time," Puck answered. The same answer the boy received since first asking a decade earlier.

Before he could press the issue, already aware of the futility, a diminutive fairy flew through the stone trees and landed on Puck's shoulder. She said something to the Fae and lifted into the air. She was a beautiful winged Sprite, with blue-green hair and completely nude. Aware of Cahal's stare, she zipped playfully around his head, hovered to jiggle ample breasts (for an eight-inch-tall-fairy) in his face, before retracing her route out of the forest.

Skerrit laughed at the boy's blushing, but Puck seemed unaware. The message distracted him from the entertainment.

"Titania requires your presence," he said to Cahal. "Now."

"What did you do to piss off the Queen?" the centaur asked.

"Nothing. I swear," he stammered in reply. "Nothing I know I did."

"You'll find out when you get there," Puck said. "She's waiting in her office. Shoo."

"Are you coming?"

"We weren't asked," the red-haired, short, muscled Fae replied. "Cahal, act respectful. Make no promises and ask no favors. Listen to whatever the Queen has to say. Do not commit yourself to any one course. Do not admit to any wrongdoing. The fewer words from your mouth the better. I will be outside the room waiting."

Apprehension turned into full-on dread. The boy nodded and ran. His Fae taking control, his speed increased significantly. Had Skerrit tried to run with him, the horse-Fae would have been left behind.

He exited the Rockforest into the late afternoon of a Tipperary day. The green pastureland of the Golden Vale stretched around him. The sky not one shade of blue, but several. White clouds made to resemble visions and dreams hung between the blue and the green. The Gaitee Mountains sat on the horizon behind him as he ran for the lowering sun and a dense tree line bordering the Vale.

The stream he jumped would eventually empty into the River Suir. Inside the live forest he began to ease his pace. At a jog he travelled well-worn trails until the trees opened onto a plateau.

The scene before him consisted of a humble village, scattered buildings of imposing size and design, and a castle, complete with fortress wall, placed on the highest point of the plain. The air above the community shimmered, creating an impression of glitter caught in a breeze. Ancient powerful magik created the glamour used to hide the capital from anyone not Fae. Sunlight streaming across the spell created the glitter effect.

Cahal slowed to a walk as the path changed from trodden dirt to cobblestones. Not every Fae lived in structures, but those who did tended to keep them in good order. Especially if yours set beside one of the streets leading to the Castle. The houses built of grey stone, with dark wooden doors, window frames, and shutters. The vast majority single story homes with a thatched roof. The occasional two-story building offered a service on the first floor -- cobbler, potions, clothier, specialty foods, cell phones -- with living quarters above.

The village of Fairies would be quaint if not for the sore thumbs sticking out and above the thatched rooflines. Most made of marble, one built of thick timbers, and one from gabbro, or commonly known as black granite. These were the mansions of the Fae Royals. Designs ran from a simplistic large square box, to

Greek temple-style including exterior columns. The fortress made of timbers belonged to Skerrit. Locals nicknamed it 'The Stable.' The dark, menacing walls of gabbro covered the smallest of the Royal manses. The capital home of Maerrighan, the Nightmare. The Fae responsible for escorting the souls of dead warriors to their spiritual home. A suitable material as black granite is often used for headstones. If not for the brooding color, the black tile shingled roof, and the darkened windows, Morgan's home would look like a Spanish hacienda.

At the highest point of the plateau, Oberon's Castle covered several acres. The outer walls built of stone, faced with blue marble. The gaping entry held mahogany doors, ten-inches thick and ready to swing closed if ordered. Cahal crossed beneath the sharpened spikes of the silver portcullis. The defensive gate would slide down to support the doors from battering. Made of silver in deference to the majority of Fae's intolerance of iron and iron alloys.

Unlike human castles, Oberon's included a massive open front courtyard where Fae could mass for celebrations or announcements. The main building, home to the King and Queen, was the only building inside the walls. It consisted of hundreds of rooms, and the deepest, darkest, most delicious dungeon.

Picking up the pace as his apprehension increased, the boy hurried up the two-dozen marble steps and entered the castle through the normal-sized door to the side of the massive formal entry. Inside he turned right and for Titania's half of the castle. She would be waiting in her office.

A few sprites skittered about, but the normally busy corridors less hectic this day. The fall of his footsteps resounded loud as gunshots in the tranquility. Arriving at the Queen's official office, unsure of the proper protocol, he knocked and waited.

"Go in."

The voice, though familiar, startled him, pressing the air he did not realize lay captured in his lungs out in a huff. His knees nearly buckled.

Morgan, dressed in black leather and looking both beautiful and dangerous as always, pressed her hand against the oak door, pushed it open and entered. Cahal, heart in throat, followed.

Titania sat behind a desk, a white-feather quill busy scratching notes on a pad while her eyes scanned the screen of a current-model IBM desktop computer. The Queen looked up to nod at her visitors, and returned to her notes.

Cahal, six-inches shorter than Morgan, and well aware of the difference, kept his attention on Titania. He tried hard to not notice the floral scent of 'The Crow,' or how the laced vest displayed a generous amount of side-view boob.

Titania was equally beautiful, with dark auburn hair and almond-shaped eyes. She did not exude the sultry of the Maerrighan.

"Cahal."

The Queen saying his name pulled him away from thoughts of sultry, and back into the sunlit office.

"It has been decided you will continue your education in London with the vampire, Bishop," she announced. "Morganna and Puck will escort you. Pack. A car will take you to the Shannon airport. You should arrive in London soon after sundown."

Titania returned to her note-taking.

"How long will I be studying in London?" he asked. Hurriedly adding, "So I know how much to pack."

"Pack it all," the Queen answered. "You'll be there for the foreseeable future."

In the hallway, the boy turned to the Fae and said, "I've gone to a lot of places to study, but I always knew I would be coming home again. Titania made it seem like I may not be coming back."

"'Foreseeable future' she said," Morgan said. "You may only be half-Fae, Cahal Kearney, but this will always be your home. Now go pack. Put anything that can follow you later into one pile, and only things you need into luggage for the trip."

"How do I know what I really need? I have no idea what I'm going there to study. Or for how long?"

"Clothes, toiletries, books, and weapons," she answered. "What more could a young man need?"

Chapter 3

"The most difficult part occurred at the cave entrance," Cale said. "When I unfolded the bodybag I'd left there, Arina refused to get in. The idea of being hauled around in a sack upset her more than the Nunnehi allowing me to take her."

"I almost sympathize with her," Annabeth said. "Rising to find yourself zipped in a garbage bag is unsettling."

The vampire was transported from Africa to Canada in the front seat of a NATO jet following the death of a Blood Demon by hippopotamus. Since this occurred after sunrise, to protect her Cale placed her in a bodybag.

The redhead rocked her pelvis. The motion pushed his penis deeper. The pelvic tilts and slow rising up and down as she straddled her lover kept the friction against her clitoris constant. Following an hour of rough, demanding sex, she now wanted it slow and under her control. Deep green eyes watched his excitement grow as he watched her breasts rise and fall with each post. Her pink lips parted to reveal the cute gap between her front teeth and the extended fangs. The incisors came to fine points, capable of puncturing skin without resistance or ripping it from bone.

"With the sun rising, she had no choice," he said, his respiration quickened with her steady gyrations. He enjoyed the sight of the reddening eraser-shaped nipples high on her firm, round tits. "It was die by sword removing her head, die writhing under the sun, or get in the bag and take her chances with a trial."

"Writhing?"

"The word came to mind," he replied. His smile a result of the growing pleasure and the oddity of the conversation.

Following a nasty break-up with Annabeth years earlier, he and Arina became lovers. She pursued the relationship to gain inside information on the Council of Four. At the same time she completed plans to destroy the Council's work: to maintain order between humans, witches, vampires and the Fae.

Arina worried the unbridled development of human technology represented a danger to her and other non-humans. The twenty-thousand-year-old terrestrial vampire decided her kind should rise to the top of the food chain before the new, powerful *magic of technology* provided humans the means of subjugating the other species sharing the planet.

Humans owned a history filled with abuse of power. She aimed to take control before they began exploiting the burgeoning advantage. Witches, a sub-set of humans, represented the biggest hurdle in her path to dominance. They used real magic to protect their own.

Arina enlisted the Nunnehi to find powerful mercenaries from another dimension willing and able to murder the Legacy Witches. Cahal Kearney, the Council of Four's Enforcer, with the help of friends, a hippopotamus, and military units from around the globe, stopped the Blood Demons. In the process he uncovered Arina's plot.

"She didn't appear concerned when she came out of the bag," Annabeth said.

Annabeth and Bishop, Council of Four vampire representative, met him at the entrance to the Council's location in London. They, and a security team, accompanied the Dúnmharú to a service lift and a short descent to the subbasement. Cale placed Arina, in bag, on a bed within a nicely furnished cell. They waited as he unzipped the black bodybag.

The slender, dark-haired vampire uncoiled and rose. Nude, and without modesty, she wrapped her arms around Cahal's neck and pulled him into a kiss. When Cahal unwrapped her embrace and stepped away, she gave Annabeth a wink.

"I hope breakfast arrives soon," she said, lowering languidly to sit on the edge of the bed.

"She's keeping her cool," he agreed.

"A bit thin for my taste," the relatively young vampire said. She leaned forward, her hands resting on his chest as his gripped her ass. She sped up, lifting and lowering herself on his thick dick. His length insured he would not slip out as she rose before pushing down, higher and faster with each thrust.

Annabeth Hughes died during the London plague of 1854. She was nineteen. One-hundred-sixty-four-years later she still looked nineteen. She could wear make-up to cover her freckles, dress to accentuate her shape, and use decades of practice to appear older when she desired. She could also go on rants which made her appear to be any teenage girl on the planet. At the moment she looked like a young woman with a killer body. A woman with over one-hundred-years of experience with sex.

Cahal Kearney, half-human and half-Fae lived fewer than thirty-years. He possessed the advantages of his heritage, human and Fae, and the abilities necessary to become the Council's Enforcer. He was Dúnmharú. Assassin. Executioner. Murderer. None of which helped as Annabeth controlled him. She did not need exceptional vampire strength. She did not use her ability to mesmerize with her voice. She used the muscles in her thighs, the sight of her naked skin, and how tight he fit within her. He lasted until the sharp manicured nails dug into his chest. The orgasm rocked through his entire body, arching him on the bed. Annabeth met his with hers.

"We're going to have to shower together if we plan on making it to the Council meeting on time," she said. She remained on top.

Cale rose, making sure he stayed inside her, wrapped his arms around the slender girl, and kissed her deeply. Releasing her lips, he said, "Cold water or we'll never make it."

The walk from Bishop's home in Soho to the Council enclave near the Inner Temple Gardens took twenty-minutes. Time enough for Cale and Annabeth to tamp down the giddiness of their renewed relationship and put on game faces.

The Dúnmharú and the only other vampire allowed to reside in the United Kingdom or Ireland besides Bishop entered the administration building. The retinal scanner on the antique doors (reinforced with steel) popped the lock. From the stone and marble entry to the Council of Four's official conference room, no one impeded their path.

Cahal Kearney, dressed in a dark grey suit with a polka-dot silk tie from Drake's, strode with purpose. Annabeth Hughes, wearing a Paris-designer business-skirt outfit of navy-blue with stiletto heels and a pure white Italian satin blouse, moved as an air-elemental witch would, flowing across the marble floor. A power couple comfortable with people staying out of their way.

Cahal followed Annabeth into the chamber. In the front of the room, a centuries-old wooden Judge's-style bench rested on a raised platform. This particular bench long enough to sit four comfortably. Unlike a court where one expected rows of pews, the space before the Council's bench offered comfortable leather club chairs.

Robert Turner, the Council's Chief of Security, rose to greet them. Early fifties, tall and solid. Former Royal Marine, former London Metropolitan Police Assistant Commissioner, and Assistant Director General of MI-5 before Bishop hired him away to oversee the Council's vast security network. He presented Annabeth with a handshake and a smile. Equals. He and Cahal exchanged forearm-locks. Brothers-in-arms.

"They've been mucking about for fifteen-minutes," he told them. "Waiting on someone in communications to confirm a sat-link to the States."

The Council of Four consisted of representatives of the four species and races sharing the planet. Representatives not to be taken literally. These four made decisions that crossed over boundaries to insure equality of treatment by and between the different beings.

"I see Phiona is representing the Fae," Cahal said. "A Fionnghuala Fae. A strong believer in communications and sorority. She'll have a direct line to Titania," the half-Fae said.

"I thought she was Annabeth when I first walked in," Turner said. "Slender, red hair, and green eyes. Could be your sister."

"I wish I was that beautiful," Annabeth replied. "Her outfit is gorgeous. A dress made from spun silver with white feathery puffs on the shoulders."

"Phiona can change into a swan," Cahal said. "She wears silver armor lighter than air. You're seeing her glamoured version. The quill she has in her fingers represents her symbol, the white feather."

"General Sarcone is bitching about the time," Turner said, turning their attention to an older gentleman seated beside the lovely Fae. "He's been the human rep on the Council for a decade and still cannot stand the majority of meetings happening at night."

"You would think he would expect it considering vampires are represented," Annabeth said.

The General noted Cahal's presence with a short nod before returning his attention to Phiona.

"Has she placed a spell on him?" Turner asked. "Sarcone is not particularly fond of the Dúnmharú concept."

"He was perfectly fine with employing an executioner," Cahal responded. "His problems were with me. The way we cooperated with military units to stop the Blood Dragons may have swayed him . . . a little. I don't recognize the witch."

"Tabath Wray, Spellcaster," Annabeth said. "She lives here in London. I'm surprised the witches have not tapped her before to represent them on the Council. The Legacy Witches have the strongest powers, and no one would consider moving on any action without consulting them first, but Tabath might be the exception."

The fair-skinned young woman stood with her hands in the pockets of her cream-colored pant-suit. The deep v-neck displayed an ample cleavage, and the suit's belt accentuated a petite waist. Wavy mahogany tresses framed a narrow face and fell to her shoulders. Blue eyes watched the three of them and her pinched lips indicated a sour taste.

"She doesn't appear to like us," Cahal said.

"You," Annabeth corrected. "Actually, your grandmother, Simone."

Simone Sinclair, Cahal's maternal grandmother, was a Legacy Witch. An air-elemental who controlled the portal at Hellam, Pennsylvania from her home in Quebec City, Canada.

"I don't think Simone has ever done anything specific to cause Tabath to hate her. It's more like a general Spellcaster-hate-Legacy kind of disdain. You're getting some of the overflow," the vampire finished.

The final person on the raised platform appeared to be a forty-something urban professional. Banker or literary agent. Well-dressed and neatly groomed. The type of man you noticed for a moment and forgot a moment later. The eldest non-terrestrial vampire on the planet, and the de facto head of the Council of

Four, as well as the Vampire Directorate, which directly governed vampire affairs.

Cahal noted the ear-piece when Bishop nodded at nothing and spoke to no one.

"We can begin," the vampire-in-charge said, having received the message he needed.

The Four Council Members took their positions facing the three visitors, who each took a chair. A high-def screen on the wall to Bishop's left came on, and another person joined the meeting.

"Everyone here knows Jace Burrell."

The olive-skinned, handsome man on the screen had slicked back black hair, and black eyes beneath dark brows. A slightly hooked nose made him appear birdlike, in a predatory bird way. One of the surviving five non-terrestrial vampires following the human-vampire war, his region consisted of North, Central, and South America. Arina was his first convert. The first terrestrial vampire turned by him, and presented the southeastern section of North America as her diocese within his domain. Of course, twenty-thousand-years-earlier these areas were not known as the Americas. Times, and names, change. Back then Jace Burrell was known as SSara Den.

"I know this meeting was called to discuss the trial of Arina Kishka," he said from the wall, forgoing any pleasantries. "I have a more pressing problem, and one I could use the Council's help resolving."

"Should we ask our guests to leave?" Bishop asked, indicating Turner, Annabeth, and Cahal.

"No. They can hear, and would have been told soon enough," Burrell answered. "Arina's betrayal has been one in the works for over a century. Her growing distaste for anyone not a vampire has been an issue for centuries. This, and the fact none of the oldest of vampires have ever been removed from their positions created a power void in her diocese. I have no way of determining if any of the vampires under her domain can be trusted. If she is executed, there will be demands to replace her, but I cannot know who would not try and carry on her treason."

"Sounds like you need to take over yourself," General Sarcone said. "It's your area to control. Control it."

"Those who fled with Arina into the Nunnehi underground have returned to Atlanta," Burrell continued, ignoring Sarcone's suggestion. "They are marshaling other vampires, as well as hundreds of thralls and humans to join them. My understanding is they intend to launch a bloody attack against humans and witches, even Fae if they get in the way. Unless you free Arina."

"I say again, Burrell," Sarcone interrupted more loudly. "Get down there and take command."

"It will cause a vampire-on-vampire war," Bishop said. "If Arina's coterie was going to meekly sign on to Jace's decisions, it would have already happened. Her lieutenants intend to force her release by threatening to bring the eyes of the world onto vampires."

"People already know vampires exist," Tabath said. Her voice honey. The perfect tone and cadence for a top-level Spellcaster. "Just as they know of witches and the Fae."

"Know and ignore," Phiona said. "Humans have a way of accepting and then dismissing anything they cannot fully comprehend. This quality allows non-humans to share the world with minimal friction or interference."

"If a vampire blood-orgy occurred in a city the size of Atlanta, the news would shake the entire planet," Bishop added. "Every media outlet would play scenes of mutilated bodies and ask if this was only a first step."

"I could rush down there with my own vampires, but the battles would be epic," Burrell said.

"All the news would show is more vampire attacks," Bishop said. "We either have to turn Arina over to them, which we will not do, or we stop them without other vampires helping."

"Bad idea," Phiona said, her feather quill wiping the air in front of her. "If Arina's vampires kill people, and no vampire is seen standing against them, you still create the image of vampires as evil. SSara Den must name Arina's successor. This successor must lead the forces sent to restore order."

"Arturo Calderon is my second turned. He is in South America. Perhaps one of his lieutenants, but I do not know if any has the power to replace someone like Arina," Burrell replied.

"One last time," Sarcone interrupted again. "The Council will deal with Arina Kishka, but the power vacuum is a vampire problem. I move we turn the issue over to the Vampire Directorate."

"I must agree with the General," Tabath said. "I second the motion and vote for it as well."

"It does appear the Vampire Directorate is better suited for responding to a potential vampire uprising," the Fae added. "If it becomes an actual uprising, and it spills across to harm non-vampires, then the Council can reconsider our involvement. Three votes for placing this with the Directorate. This means you, Bishop."

"I realize my responsibilities," Bishop replied. "I also agree vampires need to police our own before turning to the Council. Since Jace is already connected, if I can have use of the conference room, I will continue the conversation as the head of the Vampire Directorate, not as a member of the Council of Four."

Sarcone left quickly, followed by the witch, Tabath. She gave a parting smile to Bishop, and a scowl for Annabeth and Cahal.

Phiona seemed to float from the room. She stopped and gave Annabeth an unexpected embrace.

"Sister, you are blossoming with age. Make sure you do not forget wisdom is a weapon also." To Cahal she said, "You have powerful allies among the Fae Royals. With such friends, one must expect to attract powerful enemies. You are Dúnmharú, but you are also only a kit compared to the rest of the non-humans. Please try to survive long enough to reach your potential."

As the Fae exited, leaving Annabeth and Cahal attempting to discern any hidden communications within her words, Robert Turner joined them.

"If the Council is out of the picture, I'm not needed," he said. "You have people around you who consider you both more than co-workers. If you need help, ask. I'm sure something can be done, though it may be unsanctioned."

They both thanked the Security Chief.

The two turned back to see Jace Burrell, nee SSara Den, waited patiently thousands-of-miles away. Bishop sat at his place, deep brown eyes set on them. Actually, set directly on his ward.

"We need to place someone in command of Arina's territory," he said. He turned his head to the viewing screen. "It can be a temporary position while you consider your long-term options," he said to his fellow non-terrestrial vampire. "It must be someone strong enough to fight and win against any of the turned vampires. It must also be someone with the pedigree to deserve the position. Thralls and human followers respect lineage more than older vampires. Give them a proper leader and they will follow."

"I agree, Bishop," Jace answered. "As I said, I'm not sure I have a lieutenant up to the job."

"I recommend you name Annabeth Hughes your Overlord," Bishop said.

Before Annabeth could voice an opinion, Cahal grabbed her forearm. He held her, his expression telling her to wait and listen.

"She's your first turned, not mine," Burrell said.

"My only turned," Bishop responded. "The ward of the Head of the Vampire Directorate. The blood of the origins. As powerful as any of the first terrestrial vampires, and possibly an equal fighter to those of us who came through the gates. She is a mystery to many of the vampires, thrall, and followers around the world. And the appointment is temporary."

"Bishop's daughter," Burrell said aloud. The moniker not often spoken aloud, but one given to the redhead soon after she became the only other vampire allowed to live on the British Isles. Bishop's Law. "Jace Burrell's Temporary Overlord of the Southeastern Territory. I like it."

"I'm not sure I do," she said, pulling away from Cahal restraining grip. "Actually, I'm sure I do not."

"She needs to get here soon," Burrell said, ignoring Annabeth's objection. "It's eight p.m. now. Put her on one of your fancy jets and she can be in Atlanta before sunrise. I can make the announcement, set her up in a safe place, and by sunset tomorrow she can begin cleaning house."

"I'll call you with the final flight details," Bishop promised, turning away from the already-dark screen.

"I really don't get a say?" she asked.

"Considering everything, You would agree . . . eventually," he replied. "We don't have the time for eventually. Cahal has a home on an island three-hundred miles from Atlanta. Maggie Giamonte is in Quebec and can be in Atlanta to help you set up in hours. Simone Sinclair is the Legacy Witch for the same territory you will be in charge of restoring, and she's your oldest friend."

"Simone is your oldest friend." Cale made the statement sound like a question. A troubled question. "You and my grandmother are bffs. Was anyone planning on telling me? And how did this happen? When did it happen?"

"A long time before you were born," Annabeth answered.

"And something you can discuss later," Bishop added. "The point I'm making is you have support in place. More importantly, you have the ability to take command of the situation and do it before Arina's coterie creates havoc."

"I agree," Cale interjected. "The sooner you can get there, the more likely you can prevent the vampires and their people from causing harm. The quicker you establish dominance, the better."

The vampire with the face of a college co-ed and the eyes of age turned those eyes on the two people she trusted above all others.

"Temporary Overlord only," she said to her sire.

"Until Jace can place a suitable candidate before the Directorate," Bishop replied.

"You're coming to Atlanta," she said to Cale.

"I had to go back to rebuild my house," he answered. "I can bounce between Hilton Head and Atlanta with no problem."

"Call Burrell and tell him I need a house," she ordered the unofficial leader of vampires on the planet. "Not a condo, and not in the suburbs. A house with lots of rooms, ample yard, high walls, the latest security systems, and a helicopter pad would be a plus. I need space for Maggie, and the yard is for Daegen. He can stay with me since Cale's house is useless."

"Getting something like that close to downtown might be difficult, but I'm sure Jace has the contacts. Even at this time of night. Anything else?" Bishop asked.

"I need to get home and pack. We'll need a Council jet ready. And I want Michele Quan. Not only to drive me to the airport. I want her with me in Atlanta."

"Michele works for the Council's security team," Bishop replied. "The Council turned this over to the Vampire Directorate. Turner may not be able to assign his top agent to you."

"Then have the Vampire Directorate hire her away from the Council," Annabeth countered.

Bishop smiled, his fangs turning the moment into devious delight. "I'm already acting without the actual consent of the Directorate," he said. "Might as well spend their money, too. I'm sure Ms. Quan will not be cheap."

4:10am RAF Mildenhall

The Council's fastest jet was located at the private civilian air transportation hangars adjacent the Mildenhall RAF base. The mixed-use airport handled commercial flights, private aircraft, and NATO military aircraft. The airfield, eighty-miles north of London, required only a short helicopter flight.

The two jumped from the ferry chopper with bags in hand. A ground crew scurried to unload crates and cases from the cargo bay, placed them on a trolly, and transferred everything to a waiting Gulfstream G650.

The aircraft company's largest business-class jet could hold up to eighteen passengers. It was Gulfstream's fastest twin-engine craft, with a top end of Mach 0.925. At over sixty-six-million-dollars, interior design engineers would configure the jet to the new owner's personal wishes.

The two watched the handlers store the cases and secure the cargo door before taking the steps up and into the spacious airframe.

Kristy Nichol welcomed them aboard and secured the stairway-door behind them.

The Council co-pilot first met Cale when he and Anu Talvi, Legacy Witch, flew to the portal at Houska Castle in the Czech Republic.

She brushed aside hair, cut to hang over her left eye, to see into his dark eyes.

"I hope you plan on staying on board for the entire trip this time," she said. "Jumping out over the Atlantic Ocean might not be the best idea."

"No jumping out this time," he answered. "This is Annabeth Hughes. Annabeth, this is Kristy Nichol. Kristy was the co-pilot when I picked up Anu Talvi."

Nichol took Annabeth's hand in greeting and said, "Of course I know who you are. Glad to have you aboard, Ms. Hughes."

"Annabeth," the redhead replied. "What's our time to Atlanta?"

"Once we're up we'll cruise at five-hundred-eighty mph. Atlanta is forty-two-hundred-miles. Touch-down in seven-and-one-half-hours. Time will be 6:45am local."

"The sun rises around 6:30am this time of year," Cale said. "We need a little more cushion."

"We're flying light," the pilot said, speaking aloud as she ran numbers in her head. "Two passengers and minimal cargo. We can push it to five-ninety, but we only gain twenty to twenty-five extra minutes. If we hit any headwinds or bad weather, the savings go away quickly."

As they discussed the time issue, the pilot moved the G650 from the taxiway toward the airstrip. The signal light warned Nichol she needed to take her seat in the cockpit, and for the passengers to strap into seats.

The Fae-human and the vampire took the first two lounge chairs and fastened seat belts.

Cale pulled out his cell, made a Facetime call, and connected the feed to the hd monitor on the forward hull.

Maggie Giamonte's face filled the screen as the wheels of the jet left the tarmac.

"I thought I was through with vampire-hours when I left London," she said. "It's eleven-thirty, and I'm in bed."

"I need your help," Cale said.

His voice elicited an excited bark and his black German Shepherd, Daegen, jumped in front of Maggie's head.

"Hi, Dae," he said. "I'll be seeing you soon, but I need to talk with Maggie."

"He misses you," the thirty-something blonde techie said, gently pushing the long head aside. "What's up?"

"Pull up weather data for the Atlantic, especially wind patterns. We're on our way from London to Atlanta and a tail-wind could make the difference between landing before or after sunrise."

"It's the beginning of hurricane season. You have a decent chance for an easterly wind," Maggie replied. "Can't guarantee it."

"You can't, but Simone can," he answered. "Show her what's in the atmosphere, plot the jet with the gps signal from my cell, and ask her if she can magic a little push."

"Smart," the tech said. "What's the point of having a grandmother who is also an Air Elemental witch if you can't ask her for a blow."

Cale started to comment on Maggie's choice of words, but the screen blanked as his handler signed off to work on the problem.

Annabeth held her hand over her mouth, stifling giggles.

"She didn't mean it that way," he said.

"I know, but that makes it even funnier. I know Simone is your grandmother, but she is also an attractive woman. And a witch. I've seen kinkier relationships."

"Speaking of relationships. We have a few hours. Tell me the story behind you and Simone being best friends."

The vampire unbuckled and rose. The jet came with a private kitchen, stocked bar, complete bath and shower, and a master-sized bedroom in the rear. It also held hidden compartments with weapons, extra clothing, and electronics. Annabeth mixed herself a whiskey sour and returned with an iced vodka for him.

"I'd rather take advantage of the bedroom, but I suppose I should stroke your curiosity instead."

She swiveled her chair, placed the lounge position back a notch for comfort, sipped her drink, and began her story.

Chapter 4

1856. London. Soho.

"We're going to have a visitor for a few days," Bishop said. He had sent Geoffrey, his butler and aide, to ask Annabeth to join him in the study.

The sullen teenager stood a few feet inside the spacious room. Her red hair hung loose to her shoulders. She rested her chin on her chest, green eyes watching the vampire behind the wooden desk.

"I realize you're still having difficulty adjusting, but I'm going to request you try and act a bit less mopey," he said.

The chin rose and the green irises became rimmed in red.

"Adjusting?" The word an accusation. "I'm a vampire. I drink blood to survive. My family is afraid of me. My friends hate me. I can-noh go into sunlight. The only people up when I'm awake are you and blokes up to no good. What more adjusting do I need?"

"Would you rather be dead?"

"Don't know," she shot back. "Didn't have a go at being true-dead."

"You had a *go* at being sick and dying," he reminded her. "The Soho plague racked you. Do you remember?"

"I do," she admitted, eyes lowering. "'Twas awful."

"More than awful. When I found you, you said you did not want to die. There was so much more you wanted to learn."

"Delirious," she muttered. "Fever. Hashing and shitting myself."

"You were destined to become a special person, Annabeth," the ancient non-terrestrial vampire said. "You now have the time to become anything you wish. The world is available to you in a way it could never be to a human. I've seen you visiting the museums at night. I watched you read books you never could have owned selling flowers on the street. Does none of this make you a little excited?"

"It's everything I dreamed of as a girl, and nothing I could ever imagine. And it's all happening at the same time. I don't know who I am. I don't know what I am."

The slumped shoulders spoke of the weariness the teenager felt. Bishop wanted to make her transition easier, but he could not. He had thousands of years watching other terrestrials turned. Some moved easily into their altered existence. Most of these lived for centuries as servants, and then thralls before turning. Some never adjusted, going insane and being put down. Most were like Annabeth. They needed to find their path in their own way. In Bishop's opinion, those who were coddled always lacked grit. Those who found the inner strength to power through the doubts associated with discovering a redefined life proved to be the strongest of the new vampires. Few were turned while close ties to family and friends existed. The time required to move from servant, to thrall, to trusted potential lieutenant often lasted centuries.

"For a few days I need you to be Annabeth Hughes," Bishop said. "I will also need for you to wear the clothes Ms. Stanesby-Lowe purchased for you. I have arranged for a local hairdresser to visit after sundown. Once our guest departs, you may return to your wallow."

"Annabeth Hughes, the poor cockney who sold flowers and lived with five brothers and sisters in one room?"

"Annabeth Hughes who sold flowers to help feed those siblings from the time she was five-years of age," Bishop countered. "The girl who sold me a red carnation because she thought England's only vampire needed more color. The young woman who watched how the upper-crust acted, dressed, and lived while she marketed her goods. The person who took a book a week in exchange for a fresh flower. The girl who stayed until after sunset to make the arrangement work."

"You still blame yourself," she said.

"I blame the men who hurt you," he answered. "I blame myself for not warning people to leave you alone before they forced you into an alley."

"Why have you always looked after me, Bishop? Why me?"

"Potential, Annabeth," he answered. "I see potential."

"Who is your guest?" she asked, seemingly changing the subject. Showing the stones that always brought her back to her feet as a child.

"Our guest is Simone Sinclair from Paris. You may have read the news about her grandmother, Rachel Campbell."

"The Legacy Witch who died in the Colonies," the young vampire said.

"Pennsylvania, in the United States," he replied. "She was the Legacy there for nearly three-hundred years. The magic finally found a host in Simone. She's twenty-one, a talented Spell Caster, and, apparently, extremely upset over leaving France for Pennsylvania."

"Must she live in the States?"

"She will be responsible for the portal in Hellam, Pennsylvania. She must be nearby to answer a request for entry. Rachel lived among the Iroquois Indians when she first received the Legacy. It was one-hundred-years before a township was built near the gate. It remains a small, isolated village. Maybe two-thousand people."

"Bockers. No wonder she's upset," Annabeth said. "Paris to wilderness. That sounds worse than going from flower-girl to vampire. At least I still get to live in London."

Bishop refused to smile, but felt relief brought about by his ward's sense of humor. Her quips and wry examination of the people around her first caught his attention. The snarky return provided hope she would regain her personality as she accepted her vampiric nature.

"Simone is demonstrating the qualities of an Air Elemental," he continued. "She is working with an Air Elemental Legacy now. I asked she spend time here as a way to inform her about the Council of Four, the history of the Legacy Witches and Vampires, and introduce her to the Fae."

"Fae will be coming, too?"

"Two or three," he answered. "We don't want to overwhelm the young woman. It is important she realizes she is not alone when she's stuck in the Pennsylvania woods."

The carriage arrived at Bishop's house, shocks compressed and horses winded from the number of luggage trunks strapped atop and to the rear of the wagon.

Bishop, Annabeth, and Geoffrey waited on the portico at the top of the half-dozen steps leading up from the sidewalk. Gas lights lit the entry of the three-story building. Gas-powered street lamps provided illumination in front of the house.

They watched the coachman's assistant hurry down from the seat and around to hold the door open for the passenger. He provided a hand for the young woman.

A black ankle boot rested on the folding step, followed by a glimpse of white lace beneath a periwinkle blue dress. Next emerged an incredibly small waist below an hourglass chest. The woman floated from the carriage to the street. Her movements so graceful, she appeared to defy gravity.

"She's lovely," Annabeth whispered.

The young woman wore her light honey-colored hair parted in the middle, smoothed over her ears, and braided into a bun at the back of her neck. She did not wear a hairnet or a bonnet. Her eyes scanned the sidewalk before turning to gaze up at the people awaiting her. As Annabeth said, a lovely face. Not a beauty. If she tried, she could have made herself beautiful. Her lack of makeup and jewelry enhanced her fine skin. Simplicity made her cupid-bow lips appear pouty, and allowed high cheeks and a strong chin a softer quality.

Geoffrey moving down the steps signaled others waiting in the stairwell leading to the basement to join him for the task of fetching luggage. It would need to be carried to the guest quarters on the third floor.

Simone nodded at the butler as she passed. Once again, she gave the impression of floating up and over the granite steps, rising toward the vampires standing before the open doorway.

As she reached the final step, she either misjudged the height of the step, or caught a boot in the linen petticoat. Regardless the reason, the French witch barreled head-long into a surprised British vampire, and the two females twisted, turned, and tumbled backward. Annabeth landed on her arse on the marble tile of the foyer. Simone landed atop Annabeth.

The blonde, her hair less perfect, pushed herself up so her face no longer pressed against the redhead's bosom.

"MERDE!" she said. "I cannot walk worth damn with all of this air lâche."

"At least you landed on something soft," Annabeth responded. "My arse is going to be black and blue."

Bishop, recovered from the startling accident, lifted Simone, placing her, standing, on the tile. He gave his arm to Annabeth, who used it to lift herself.

"Are you harmed?" Bishop asked Simone.

"My ego may never recover," she answered. "Thank you for catching me," she said to Annabeth. "I am Simone Sinclair, awkward Air Elemental witch."

"Annabeth Hughes, vampire-in-training."

Annabeth's story was interrupted by the pilot coming back to the cabin.

"Tom Farway," Cale said, rising to shake hands with the man. "Haven't flown with you in ages."

"Glad to have you aboard," the black man said. His smile reflected his genuine appreciation. "The first time was a hell of an adventure. And welcome to you also, Annabeth."

"Hello, Tom." Annabeth remained in her seat. "I've flown with you several times. What's this adventure with Cale?"

"My first job as Dúnmharú," the younger man answered. "Stuff for another time. How's our time?"

"Picked up one strong tailwind. We may top Mach One the way it's pushing us. ETA Atlanta is currently six o'clock in the morning. Should give us at least a thirty-minute window before sunrise. The other reason I came back was to pass along a message. Quan is aboard a jet and following. She should reach Atlanta a couple of hours after us."

"We have a lengthy flight ahead and plenty of food and space back here," Cale said. "If you and Kristy want to take breaks, don't hesitate."

"We'll begin rotations in an hour," the pilot replied. "Right now I want to keep an eye on the weather. Our tailwind wasn't in the forecast."

"Don't stress the wind," Cale said. "I have a good source for weather updates. I predict our breeze will be with us the entire way."

Farway began to comment, considered who spoke, accepted his prediction, and returned to the cockpit.

"Tell me more about you meeting Simone," he said, returning to his seat.

Annabeth's story was interrupted again. This entrance required no doors.

Morgan appeared in the center of the cabin, her materialization causing the air pressure to change, popping ears.

"I require you," the dark haired, dark eyed Fae said to Cale. "I'm calling in your debt."

Cale, hand clasped over his nose, blew air to unblock his ears. "What did you say?"

"You asked me for a favor. I'm here for repayment," she repeated. "Now."

"I can't go now," he protested, standing. "Annabeth needs me."

He fell to his knees. Eyes wide, hands to his chest. A scream caught in his throat.

"What are you doing to him?" the vampire demanded. "Stop it!"

"I'm doing nothing," Morgan answered. "He's trying to deny a favor given for payment to a Fae. This is the penalty. If he continues, he will die."

The Fae drifted forward and knelt beside the struggling half-Fae.

"Listen, Cahal Kearney. You will repay me or you will die. Will your death help Annabeth?"

He tried calling on his darker soul; his Fae. The result caused the pain to increase. With no other choice, he nodded at the Maerrighan in agreement, letting his sweat-soaked forehead drop to the cabin floor.

Annabeth dropped to her knees beside Cahal,. She massaged his shoulders and spoke quietly in his ear. The words had no meaning, but the emotions did. She would be okay. He needed to relax. The mantra repeated until he could take a deep breath. His head cleared, and his muscle control returned.

Standing, he said, "I promised a favor. What do you want?"

"First, you must come with me to Oberon's Castle," the Royal said. "The King has returned and there is a problem I need your help solving."

"Annabeth?" he asked.

"I will see she receives help. This is not a favor for a favor. Keeping the vampires under control is important to all who share this world. If humans become fearful of non-humans, there will be no world to share."

Kristy hurried from the cockpit to discover the redheaded teenage vampire standing alone.

"We thought we had a cabin pressure leak," she said. "Is Cale in the back?"

"He's gone," the vampire answered. "The pressure change was a Fae Royal transporting in and out. He left with her."

"Damn," the co-pilot said. "One day I'm going to start a flight with that man on board and actually land the plane with him still on board."

Chapter 5

Morgan materialized on the western lawn of Oberon's Castle. Cahal dropped to his knees and vomited. The same reaction as the first time she transported him. Realizing it might happen again, she opted for a private, outdoor location to land. Puking on the castle's marble tiles would not have been becoming.

Rising, pale, but under control, he asked, "I don't suppose you would tell me what favor you need before we go inside?"

"King Oberon returned," she said.

"You told me that on the plane."

"For the last few centuries he has been making periodic quests through the dimensions looking for signs of Pandaemonium," she added.

"He's looking for chaos?"

"The name has become synonymous with chaos, as Bedlam Hospital for the insane also became a word for chaos," Morgan answered. "Pandaemonium is a place. It is a world created by the Dark Queen of the UnSeelie. A hidden place where she creates her own version of Fae. A dark version; evil and hate-filled creatures with cruel natures. Oberon heard whispers from travelers she is preparing for an attack on the Fae. She has been sending scouts into the portal gates for millennia, trying to find the path back here."

"Back here? She's been here?"

"She was betrothed to Oberon," the Fae spirit guide answered. "Before they were joined he fell in love with Titania, the daughter of Titans. In her anger she attempted to kill Titania. He could not destroy her. He felt responsible for the pain which became her murderous rage. He banished her to a world in another dimension."

"If he left her, why is he searching for Pandaemonium? He should know where it is."

"She did not stay there, Cahal. She left, found another world better suited for her long-term plans. Pandaemonium is an ancient myth from Fae history. If Oberon is correct, she settled and began creating UnSeelie to turn the myth into reality. When she amasses an army large enough, and her scouts locate a path to Earth, she will return. The war she brings with her will be waged against every living thing on this planet and on Tir na Nog, our home world."

"The gates are warded with magic," he countered. "She would be barred."

"You recently killed two plane-travelers who used magic to break through a warded entrance," Morgan reminded him. "Blood Dragons are nothing compared to the magic available to the Dark Queen. The portals will fall before her."

"I still don't get what favor I can provide."

"Oberon traveled with a warrior. His body guard and companion. He traveled with your father, Sionnach Catharnagh. He did not return with him."

"The King left my father in Pandaemonium? Why?"

"The answer is inside the castle," she answered.

The slender woman changed as she turned toward the edifice. Her black satin dress became an armored vest of the same black shade. Greaves of brass covered both forearms. A pleated leather skirt covered her to mid-thigh, and leather knee-boots with flat heels completed the transformation.

Her black tresses were pulled back and held with a brass clasp. A leather choker circled her neck. As he watched, a black cape of gossamer cloth settled over her shoulders and hung to an inch above the ground. She pulled it closed to cover the deep cleavage created by the vest pressing her breasts together and up.

"No blade? No bow?" he asked.

"Not for meeting with the King," she answered. "Cahal, Titania likes you. Your entire life the Royals have treated you as one of their own. You are family, but you have never been before Oberon. His last quest began shortly after your birth. It is why you have no memories of your father. You must contain your emotions before the King."

"I remember my court training," he replied.

"This is one-thousand-fold the laws of court," she answered. The serious tone held his attention. "Your best defense is to say nothing. Ask nothing. Agree to nothing. If a question is asked directly to you, I will try to answer for you. If I am not allowed, I want you to answer honestly, but use as few words as possible."

"The simple truth," he said.

"Fae carry no concept of simple truth, Cahal Kearney," she said. "Say too much and you could place yourself into slavery. Say something with a smart-mouth and you could be chained in a dungeon for hundreds of years. Question any action or the authority of Oberon and you will be killed. Slowly. No Fae will stand up for you. Do you understand?"

"Stay cool, stay quiet," he answered. "Am I dressed okay?"

He wore a long-sleeve tactical shirt, black, tucked into cargo pants of dark grey. His laced boots were actually side-zipped and a lightweight design created by Belleville Khyber. All of his weapons remained in cases 42,000ft over the Atlantic Ocean.

"You look dangerous," she said. "Which is appropriate."

Cahal followed Morgan through a side entrance. The corridors of the castle familiar from his youth when he spent hours exploring the massive citadel. Everywhere from the ground floor and up. Areas below ground level were off limits. They walked a hallway leading to the public rooms on the first floor. Chambers for assemblies, meeting rooms, and dining facilities used when groups of Fae gathered. The court and auditorium for adjudicating disputes waited at the end of the wide hallway.

Fae walked, slithered, and flew in both directions. Some congregated for whispered conversations. Cahal noticed the lack of buzz. When Fae gathered the air would normally be filled with chatter. Folk were famous for their camaraderie. They rarely allowed an opportunity to tell stories and brag of accomplishments to pass. Other than the few sotto voce confabs, everyone else appeared in a hurry, but without any specific destination. All moved aside as Morgan marched forward, Cahal a step to her right and slightly behind.

She stopped at a door twelve-feet high and covered with gold filigree. The door would take them to a smaller chamber. Morgan turned to the hybrid and pressed a finger to her lips as a final reminder. She pressed her hand against a golden faceplate and entered.

The Seomra Ríoga, the Royal Room, was the only round chamber within the castle. It had stone walls without windows, a single door, and a massive round table without a center. Cahal always thought of Camelot and the Arthurian Tales when entering this space.

Ten chairs were occupied. In his lifetime, the half-human, half-Fae could not recall a time when a meeting of Royals filled all ten spots. A quorum of six could enact policies that affected a cross section of Folk, or between the Fae and the other races.

Skerrit sat in front of the door. The centaur, in his humanoid form, did not turn to see who entered.

Morgan walked left, crossing behind Ainnir Isce, the leader of water Fae. A young woman with pale skin and white hair. She cast her aqua-blue eyes toward the pair, but made no other sign of interest.

Fin Bheara, dressed in black, with his hair slicked back, sporting a three-musketeer mustache and goatee, turned in his seat to watch the Maerrighan. He actually licked his lips. His eyes locked on the exposed upper breasts of the warrior-Fae. He ruled the most heroic warriors among the Seelie. Morgan one of the few not beneath his command, and not beneath him in a bed. Bheara, married to a woman considered the most beautiful of all Fae, simply could not stop himself from attempting to lay anything female.

Eoboirean sat beside Fin Bheara. The young man sat quiescent, with soft brown hair falling across his eyes as he held his chin down. He represented the woodland Fae, mainly nymphs, dryads, and those who lived among the trees. He rarely came to the capital.

Morgan took her place alongside Eoboirean. Cahal stood against the stone wall behind her position. His eyes locked on the figure to Morgan's left. Oberon. The King. The Fae ruler nodded to Morgan, and turned his dark brown eyes on Cahal Kearney. He appraised the Dúnmharú. Whatever decision he made, he kept to himself.

Titania sat by the side of her husband. The Queen's posture perfect, her hands folded in her lap beneath the table's top. She sat across from Ainnir Isce, but her gaze travelled far beyond the water Fae.

Puck stood behind Titania, as Cahal did behind Morgan. He was a Royal, but not high enough on the ladder to receive a chair in the Seomra Ríoga. The short cross between a lumberjack and a leprechaun winked as he caught Cahal's attention.

A ghost, or spirit, or wisp floated beside Puck, stationed behind the next Royal in the circle. Cahal never met Ysbaddaden, but knew him immediately. The rough brown beard and wild hair from which brooding black eyes peered from above an eagle's beak nose. He wore a grey shroud. His shoulders humped up, forcing his head to hang forward. The Royal who watched over the dead. Morgan delivered fallen spirits to their next existence. Ysbaddaden maintained order between the living, and the two dimensions of passed souls. Humans would call these places heaven and hell.

It seemed appropriate Ysbaddaden sat beside Tommy Rawhead. Also known as "Bloody Bones." He appeared a simple man in his middle ages. His eyes constantly cutting around the room. His right eye would twitch without any rhythm to the act. He looked painfully thin, with drawn face and sharp, pointed chin. He acted as the leader of Seelie who walked a thin line between sane and crazed. Few Fae would ever consider harming others, but those who do consider it must be controlled. Tommy was the Fae Boogeyman. Not exactly sane himself, but under control. When not in this glamor, he looked like a demonic scarecrow with sharp teeth and yellow eyes.

The contrast between Tommy, even in his less-frightening guise, and Phiona, the lovely red-haired nature-lover, obvious with the two seated side-by-side. She wore her silver gossamer armor and held a swan-feather, wiping it mindlessly across her chin. She smiled at Cahal when their gazes locked.

Thirteen in attendance. The Seelie year is composed of thirteen months. Thirteen full moons. The maximum number allowed inside the Seomra Ríoga.

"My fears did not equal reality," Oberon said. No formal calling to order. His rich voice, tinge with a weariness, resonated within the round walls. "The Black Queen has accomplished one of her goals. She created Pandaemonium. A world within a dark dimension filled with Fae as opposite to our race as can be imagined. It is a place of such hatred and loathing the creatures there happily murder each other."

"How, my Lord?" Fin Bheara asked. "She was a powerful Fae, but how could she create an entire world of UnSeelie?"

"I do not know every detail. I can only tell you what I have discovered. Traveling to other worlds, I heard rumors of a place described as a home for demons. I was told the foulest of beings sought it as a refuge. I believe many of the beings there are not Faerie-bred, but creatures of hate and cruelty drawn to her."

Oberon's eyes closed. He opened them, staring across the table at Skerrit.

"I saw animals of high intelligence, and vicious demeanor," he said, directing the descriptions to the Fae's greatest hunter. "A cavalry of winged, four-legged animals without hair. Reddish skin. Heads like alligators, with much longer teeth and tusks."

"Capaelliathlu," Skerrit said. "Horse-bats. They were created by Druids to fly them into battle. They were exterminated in the last Druid war. The one who controls Air and Darkness, the Black Queen, could have used the same magic."

"There were dark elves. Cursed beings from another dimension," Oberon said. "Serpents I have never seen before. Beings with humanoid bodies, but narrow skulls and mouths with hundreds of tiny, pointed teeth, yellow eyes, and long, thin tongues."

"Piast," Ainnir Isce said. "They left through a gate thousands of years ago. They could not stand being told to leave humans alone."

"I saw creatures that resembled brownies, sprites, and other Fae, but with evil reeking from their sweat," the King added. "Things not witnessed in my thousands of journeys through the portals."

"You saw these things," Phiona said. "You travelled to Pandaemonium?"

"Sionnach and I," he replied. "We followed a trail provided by a race of dwarfish people. Their village had been attacked by a group they described as tall, thin hags with vicious black dogs. After killing or injuring many of their people, these hags and hounds were driven through an exit gate. One of the dwarf leaders followed for a couple of portals. She led us to the gate she believed took the crones home. Sionnach bade me wait while he scouted the planet."

Oberon quit talking. No one interrupted his silent thoughts. He was recalling a difficult memory.

"When he returned he told me he was sure we found the Black Queen. He told me of a castle made of blackest stone. A castle built to look like this one."

"He wasn't stopped? Not attacked?" Fin Bheara asked.

"He said the creatures ignored him," Oberon replied. "It is why we decided we would both go and discover what we could. We travelled less than a mile before we were attacked. I should correct myself. *I* was attacked. The creatures came at me with vengeance and hatred. Sionnach planted himself between me and them. His sword swept through a dozen. I could see the surprise in the eyes of those left standing. They did not expect him to defend me."

"I don't understand," Ainnir said. "Why would they be surprised by Sionnach defending his sire?"

"He was invisible to them," Ysbaddaden said. His bass a rumble of gravel and grit. The sound of a voice not often used. "Many of the creatures, perhaps all of the Black Queen's subjects are magical creations. Those from other worlds have been reproducing for aeons, mixing with other beings to survive. Pandaemonium is a world of hybrids. The UnSeelie are hybrids. Sionnach Catharnagh is part-Fae. As a hybrid, the UnSeelie saw one of their own. He fit in. Oberon did not."

The Maerrighan turned sharply in her seat and raised a warning palm to stop any outburst from Cahal. Discovering his father was also half-Fae would be a shock.

His hesitation, caused by the time needed to process Ysbaddaden comments, allowed Morgan the opportunity to remind him to remain quiet. His wide eyes beseeched her for an explanation. She mouthed, "Later."

"You escaped," Morgan said.

Oberon hesitated once again. He quelled his emotions.

"An army of UnSeelie creatures arrived as we were almost to the exit. We fought them as we retreated. I entered the portal, but Sionnach stayed behind to protect me. To protect us all."

"He could not allow an UnSeelie to follow you," Titania said. "They would have discovered the gates needed to return to Earth."

Oberon nodded.

"Sionnach is either dead or captive," Bheara said. "Because you discovered her lair, the Black Queen will increase her efforts to find a way back here. She will force Sionnach to tell her the way."

"He would die first," Morgan said between clenched teeth.

"We must prepare as if she will find the way," Oberon interrupted. "If her scouts locate an entry gate to Earth, she will attack. As soon as they have destroyed this planet, they will move on to Tir na Nog. Ysbaddaden, Tommy, Phiona, Ainnir, Fin, and Eoboirean, I order you to instruct the Fae you command to begin preparations for war. Not only to defend, but be ready to repel the UnSeelie. Word will be sent to non-aligned Fae to do likewise. I also command you place sentinels at the four entry gates to Earth. Work together, but be sure each gate is watched at all times."

The King spoke to Phiona, telling her "You currently represent the Fae on the Council of Four. Inform the Legacy Witches and the Vampire Bishop of the potential for an attack by the Black Queen."

"Of course, my King," she replied. She added, "The Fae have a history of remaining neutral in wars between other races. The humans and vampires may decide to repay our past decisions to avoid taking sides by doing the same now. They may see this as a war between the Seelie and the UnSeelie, and none of their affair."

"When the Black Queen's army arrives, and it will, they will not limit their rampage to the Folk. Anyone they cross will become a victim of their cruelty. Make sure you emphasize the truth of that."

"What if the humans and vampires decide Fae are attracting a war which could sweep them into a bloody conflict and demand we leave this planet?" Ysbaddaden asked.

"I do not know," Oberon admitted. "Many of the Folk consider Earth their only home. The Black Queen will either plane-travel to Earth to reach Tir na Nog, or she will find our home world first and then attack the Fae on Earth through the passage. I doubt the crossing would be non-violent to others."

"I will warn them," Phiona said. "They need to be prepared regardless of any decision."

"Queen Titania, Skerrit, and Morrigan will stay to discuss potential strategies," Oberon announced.

"I should remain for that discussion," Fin Bheara adamantly insisted, rising from his seat. "I command the Fae warriors. As the first to fight, the plan of attack must clearly be derived from our initial actions."

"As the leader of the warriors, I want you to prepare them," Oberon replied. His tone flat, but his eyes carried a clear threat to Bheara's questioning his commands. "When time comes for strategies to become battle plans, everyone will be involved," he added.

Unhappy, Bheara tilted his head in compliance and acceptance of his King's order. The others rose and silently began to leave the room.

Cahal, unsure if he should stay or go, looked to see Puck's response. The short, stout Fae moved to follow the ghost, which hovered behind Ysbaddaden, who moved much like a wraith himself. The half-Fae took the cue, following Eoboirean toward the door.

"Cahal Kearney. Puck," Oberon called without raising his voice. "Remain with your sponsors."

Cahal looked over the expansive table at his friend, who looked back, shrugged, and made his way back to his spot behind Titania. Cahal returned to stand behind Morgan.

When the door closed behind the final Royal leaving the meeting, Oberon said, "Skerrit, sit beside the Queen. We need not shout across this table. Cahal, sit beside Morrigan, and Puck, sit by Skerrit. This meeting has nothing to do with rank or position."

With everyone seated, the King said, "We must decide how best to recover Sionnach from Pandaemonium, and stop the Un-Seelie leaving that cursed plane."

"Agreed," Titania said. "Though I am not sure how either is possible."

"Then we do what Fae have always done," Oberon said.

"The impossible," Morgan finished.

Chapter 6

The G650 touched down at the Dekalb-Peachtree Airport in Chamblee, Georgia at 6:10am local time. The private airport the only one, outside of the major Hartsfield-Jackson Atlanta International Airport, with a runway long enough to handle the big business-class jet. Fifteen-minutes from mid-town Atlanta, the less-used airfield meant less time queueing for a landing slot, a shorter taxi time to the private hangars, and transportation would be waiting when the door opened.

Jace Burrell held his hand out for Annabeth as she stepped from the lowered stairs to the tarmac. Entirely a gentlemanly gesture, as the younger vampire would have no trouble with balance.

"Welcome to the States," he said to her. "I appreciate your willingness to help me repair the damage Arina created."

Annabeth nodded and noticed Burrell's intent stare into the open hatch.

"Cahal Kearney was called away unexpectedly," she said.

"I understood he boarded with you in London," the non-terrestrial vamp said. "You certainly did not stop between Europe and here."

"As I said, it was unexpected. Fae business. They don't allow little things like international flights to get in their way."

"I do recall a certain disdain for patience," he replied, his smile dazzling and relaxed. His fangs showed, but not threatening. "It has been a long time since I had dealings with the Fae," he told her. "They are not prevalent in this part of the world."

"Except the Nunnehi," she reminded him.

"Another issue for another night," he answered. "My SUV is coated with a special UV film. If we do get caught in the sunrise, it should not be an issue. I can actually stand a bit of sunlight, if it is early or very late in the day. I don't think your lovely complexion is up to the test."

"I'd rather not find out," she said.

As they talked, baggage handlers moved cases and crates into the back of a second SUV. Tom Farway came out of the jet carrying her two bags. An automatic pistol strapped to the tall black man's right thigh.

"I'm part of your bodyguard detail," he informed both vampires. "Ex-Royal, and I stay prepared. Kristy will stay with the plane. Cale left his bags aboard. Do I get them or leave them?"

"Leave them," Annabeth answered. "If he needs anything, it will be easier for him to locate the jet than," she turned to Burrell and said, "where I'm staying?"

"Four blocks from mid-town," he answered. "Four-story pre-Civil War plantation house, fully modernized on a three-acre lot. Top-notch security system, and fully wired for electronics. The basement redesigned with a half-dozen secure rooms for over-day guests. Fifteen-minutes by car."

"Seems extremely convenient," Annabeth commented.

"It was Arina's," Burrell answered. "I hope you don't mind?"

"Not at all."

Burrell and Annabeth got into the rear of the lead SUV, with Farway taking the shotgun seat beside the driver. Quick introductions, and they discovered the driver was ex-Army Ranger and hired through a local private security firm.

The SUV following included two more private security guards. Armed and experienced.

During the short trip Burrell explained how he sent messengers and text messages to every vampire in Arina's territory informing them of Annabeth's arrival and her position as the replacement Overlord.

"I did not add temporary to the title," he said. "They best learn to live with the idea. When it is time to change, they will accept it. Arina had eight lieutenants. Three have replied and sworn allegiance to me, and through me, to you. I have not heard back from five."

"Cale said four vampires joined Arina in the Nunnehi city beneath Blood Mountain," she said.

"I have learned Arina and her coterie actively recruited servants. They exchanged blood to produce more thralls than allowed by the Vampire Directorate charter."

"We faced a couple of her younger thralls in Africa," she told him. "Not well prepared for a fight. Cale handled a number of thralls and servants on his island. They came with the female

Blood Dragon. He also killed some on Blood Mountain, before the vampires escaped."

"Untrained and unrestrained," Burrell said, disdain clear in the tone of the response. "My records show the five in question have twenty-two certified thralls, and one-hundred-eighty-six listed servants. We must assume numbers have been inflated by their unlawful recruitments. By how many? I have no idea."

The SUV caravan pulled through iron gates, opened by human guards, and continued up a driveway and directly into an expansive garage. As the automatic doors lowered, the first rays of the morning sun broke across the sky.

"Nice timing," Farway said, opening the back door for Annabeth. Burrell opened his own.

"You're beginning to doze," Burrell said, joining the listless younger vampire at the rear of the car. "I'll get you to your room now."

He took Annabeth by her arm, leading her through a doorway and into a stairwell going down. Another door, and a hallway, dimly lit. At the first door off the corridor, he opened and ushered her into a spacious room designed as an efficiency apartment might be. Farway followed, placed her bags on the floor inside the door, and retreated.

Burrell handed Annabeth a key. "This is the only key to this room. When you set the lock, you will not be disturbed until you unlock the door. You are safe. This manor is secure. I will see you after sunset."

He left, moving to another apartment down the corridor. She locked the door, placed the key on a desk, and slowly slipped off everything she wore. The darkening embraced her as the sun outside rose higher. In the queen-sized bed, beneath a sheet, she dropped into the dreamless sleep of a vampire.

"Burrell and Hughes?"

The man asking stood on a balcony. The condominiums rose fifteen-stories, and this one, on the ninth-floor, offered an unobstructed view of Arina's Plantation house and grounds.

"Must be," the woman with the telescope answered. "The SUVs had tinted windows and they drove directly into the garage. The team at the airport in Chamblee said Burrell met her at the jet and they got into the car. No where else they would have gone with the sun rising."

"Now what?"

"Wait and watch," she answered. "The Boss is down until sunset. After he rises and we confirm Burrell and Hughes are in town, then he and the others will decide what to do."

"With Arina gone and Burrell himself here, do you think they will back down?" he asked.

"Don't know a lot about the other four, but the Boss has had an itch to do something big, bad, and public for over a century," the thrall replied. "Doing it to spite an Exemplar and our newly appointed Overlord would make it bigger and badder."

"And more public."

"Worldwide," the female agreed.

Banging woke Kristy. She uncurled and placed the recliner back into a chair position. Groggy, she opened the cabin hatch and lowered the stairs for Michele Quan.

The leggy Eurasian took the stairs two-at-a-time. Kristy checked her chronometer. Ten o'clock a.m. Eastern Daylight Savings Time.

"Annabeth?" Quan asked.

"Secure in an underground apartment in a heavily guarded mansion in the middle of Atlanta," Kristy answered.

"Cale?"

"Some Fae popped in over the Atlantic and popped out with him. Annabeth wasn't concerned, so I guess leaving wasn't against his will."

"Plan?"

"Sleep to get my ass accustomed to east coast time and prepared for a vampire lifestyle," the pilot replied. "Tom is at the mansion with Annabeth. He's doing the same."

Michele closed the hatch and made her way to the bar. As she made a double scotch, neat, Kristy nestled back in her chair, pulled the blanket over, and set the recline to fully extended.

With the whiskey to help relax her, the security agent pulled a pillow and blanket from an overhead bin, found herself a chair, and set it for as comfortable as possible. The best way to overcome jet-lag and begin preparing her internal system for working on a vampire's nocturnal schedule. Booze and bed. The difficulties of working for the undead. But her new position and pay increase made the difficulties a lot less worrisome.

Banging woke the two women. Kristy came out of her sleep a bit more quickly than Michele, who woke with drool covering her chin.

"Nice look," she said to the normally beautiful woman with sand-colored skin and hair like raven-colored silk. The blanket had been pulled over her head. Her silky hair jutted out as if an electric shock zapped her.

"Shit," Michele said, trying to force her hair into something less bride-of-Frankenstein as the jet's pilot opened the hatch. Kristy jumped back to avoid being bowled over by a one-hundred-pound black German Shepherd.

Kristy first thought was wolf, and she tried to remember where the nearest weapon might be. Her second response was to smile, returning the big goofy grin the dog gave her. His tail wagged so hard, had he been near anything breakable, it would surely be destroyed.

"Damn it, Dae," Maggie Giamonte said, following the dog by actually using the stairs. "Sorry," she said to Kristy. "If I had any idea he would decide to Krypto into the plane, I would have put the leash on him. I'm Maggie and this is Dae. I'm Cale's tech support, and the dog belongs to him."

"Hi, Maggie," Michele said, coming up to join them. "DAE-DAE!" she cried in an excited girl voice, causing the big Shepherd to launch himself through her legs to present his butt for scratching. Made incredibly difficult because his body wiggled as hard as his tale wagged.

"They know each other," Maggie said to Kristy.

"No duh," replied the entertained young woman.

"I thought you were going to leave Daegen with Simone in Quebec," Michele said, lifting a shapely leg over the back of the dog to free herself from the rolling ride.

"Since I decided to come with her, it made more sense to bring him, too."

Simone Sinclair, Legacy Witch for North America, and generally considered the head of the Legacy, came through the hatch.

Kristy, a bit overwhelmed by the new arrival, backed toward the cockpit. Michele Quan, who spent several days at Simone's home in Quebec as part of the security detail sent by the Council of Four to protect her when the Blood Dragons began killing witches, moved forward to hug the stunning blonde in the most expensive business suit Kristy had ever seen.

Michele introduced the woman to the pilot, and Simone's reputation as the Ice Witch dissolved quickly. Within a minute, the Council pilot felt an affinity with the French-Canadian air elemental.

Kristy explained they were sleeping to sync their bodies to working a night-time laden schedule. She and Simone had a private laugh at Michele's expense. Her hair was totally out of control.

Simone and Maggie did not need to contend with jet-lag, already on east coast time, but decided a nap to prep for the evening was smart.

"Cale did not make the whole trip," Michele said to the arrivals.

"We know," Maggie replied. "Morgan called Simone."

"Since she shanghaied my grandson, she asked if I could arrange for Annabeth to receive additional support," Simone told them. "I felt I might qualify."

They decided Simone could have the on-board bedroom. Dae decided to join her. Maggie took a third recliner, popped in earplugs, and dropped off before Kristy and Michele could close the hatch and return to their seats.

Chapter 7

"When I returned, my first thought was to find my wife," Oberon Said. "I had not seen Titania in nearly thirty Earth years. For those who have lived longer than thousands of civilizations, it may seem a drop of water in the ocean. When it is time apart from your love and your soulmate, it is forever within an eternity."

Titania reached over the table to squeeze her husband's hand. She said nothing in response, but those with them recognized the depth of love these two immortals shared.

"Then I called for the Maerrighan. It was her husband I abandoned, and it was her quick mind and sense of strategy I needed if we are going to free him from the Black Queen."

"Oberon told me his story." Morrigan spoke with her hands clasped and resting on the table. She addressed the others without emotion. No condemnation for her King leaving her husband behind. No anger at discovering Pandaemonium existed and the dark creator planned to attack. "There is one obvious weakness among the UnSeelie."

"They overlook hybrids," Cahal said aloud. Realizing he voiced the thought, he hastened to look at Morgan, prepared to apologize for speaking at a meeting of Royals.

"It appears so," Oberon said. "Do not fear speaking your mind Cahal. When I said this meeting cared nothing for rank or position, it included you. Every thought, every idea is worthy until proven otherwise."

"You believe this because the UnSeelie are creations of magic and cross-breeding?" Titania asked.

"Yes. I do not know if she actually had sex with creatures and gave birth to some of the Dark Fae," Oberon replied. "I recognized traits of Fae and other races I thought extinct. Most destroyed by their own desire to destroy. I believe some were reconstituted using black magic. She needed subjects. In essence, these beings are hybrids. Experimentation would explain many of the others. As you say, cross-breeding."

"Anyone with partial Fae DNA would be the norm in Pandae-monium," Cahal said. "You said my father was like me. Not fully Fae. Is this true?"

"It is," Morgan answered. "Twenty-five-thousand-years ago a Fae fell in love with a Legacy Witch. She became pregnant, which is fatal for the mother, and often the child is still-born. In this case, Fae and Legacy magic were united to save the mother and the child."

"Don't leave it half told, Morrigan," The King said. "I was the Fae who sired Sionnach."

Cahal froze as Oberon's statement made its way through his mental filters. The others in the room waited, watching for the moment when . . .

"You're my grandfather," Cahal said. Realization.

"It isn't unusual for Fae to have sex with others," Titania said. "We all have, and it does not change the bonds we share. When your life is incredibly long, it is impossible not to crave fresh experiences."

"Sionnach's mother was a special person, Cahal," Morgan said. "A powerful fire elemental. She created the magic used to ward the seven portals. Before that, she and the others stood against a number of vile creatures who came through open gates and tried to harm this world. She was beautiful, and kind, and intelligent. She also had other lovers. Becoming pregnant by Oberon, The Seelie King, was deemed mythical. Everyone agreed she and the child should be saved if possible."

"Phiona and her rangers created the magic to save the Fae within her womb," Titania told him. "They are the Fae protectors of nature, and there is nothing more natural than the birth of a child."

"The twelve Legacy Witches combined the four elements to build a sphere to protect her and the child. Magic ready to inter-cede with anything either might require to survive. Fire to warm them, water to cool them, air for their lungs, and the Earth itself to make sure their hearts continued to beat," Morgan said, her eyes slightly unfocused as she remembered the time of Sionnach's birth.

"With all of that magic being thrown about, it was impossible for a mid-wife to get near," Puck said. His voice light with a touch of mirth. "The Fae can do many things, but we are inept at helping women bear children. Human mid-wives are always called upon to deliver newborn Fae. I remember to this day the look on Bishop's face when I told him he needed to mid-wife Sarah."

"Sarah?" Cahal asked.

"Sionnach's mother," Puck answered. "Bishop kneeled in the middle of enough magic to move a planet and pulled Sionnach into life. He handed him to Sarah, and a minute later all of the magic evaporated. Mother and child alive and well."

"Then I'm not half-Fae," the young man said. "I'm quarter-Fae."

"Hadn't thought about it," Skerrit, silent through both meetings until now, said. "I guess that makes you a two-bit Fairy."

He waited for someone to catch his joke. Only Cahal, who lived long enough in the United States to know a quarter-of-a-dollar was called two-bits, caught the pun.

"Good one," he said to the centaur, allowing the Hunter some satisfaction for his witticism.

"I'll explain it to the rest of you later," Skerrit said. "For now, we have established the UnSeelie have a blindspot with hybrids. How does that help us save Sionnach and stop the Black Queen?"

"We send a rescue team of our own hybrids," Morgan said. "Cahal is obvious, and since becoming the Dúnmharú, he has proven he has the ability to stand against any enemy. Skerrit, you are also part-Fae and part-Centaur. The Centaurs were once a powerful ally, and their own race. Only after centuries of co-mingling did your species become a Fae subset. Your DNA will make you appear a hybrid as well."

"And me," the Queen interjected. "My father was the last of the Titans. Titan civilization ruled Earth before the ascension of humans. I am half-Olympian and half-Titan. Sionnach has been a son to me as he was to his mother until she died. I would go to bring him back even if I were not a hybrid."

"I can see a team of three going in to search and rescue," Cahal said, more comfortable speaking before the others. "I cannot see how we could also take out the Black Queen."

"If you cannot, and you are successful at freeing Sionnach, nothing will stop her from finding her way back here and destroying everything in her path," Oberon said.

"You may be giving her way too much credit," Cahal said to his grandfather, the King.

"I know her, boy," Oberon rejoined, a tinge of aristocratic anger in his voice. "I know what she is capable of."

"I'm not questioning your knowledge, Grandfather. I'm saying you have obsessed over the potential she represented. You feel some guilt at her becoming the Black Queen by pushing her aside and marrying Titania. I also think you may forget how things have changed since she last lived on this world."

"I may be a tad biased in my opinions regarding her," Oberon admitted. "She still represents a danger."

"Agreed, and if we can stop her in Pandaemonium, we should. But if she makes the mistake of bringing her army through the portals, she will meet an enemy she is not prepared to face," the Dúnmharú said. "Humans. Humans with modern technology that rivals ancient magics. Humans with weapons unlike anything she remembers. Lead, and iron, and worse. Arina Kishka sits awaiting trial because she fears humans will supplant vampires, and possibly the Fae, as the superior race because of the advantages technology have provided."

"He's correct," Morgan said. "We have always kept Fae business within the confines of the Fae. We stood aside as neutral every time other races went to war. We never consider being a true ally to one side and risking a loss. Because of this, we never consider another race coming to our side. If the UnSeelie attack, the Seelie will stand against them, and we might best these hybrid imitations. With vampires, humans, and witches at our side, there will be no question of victory."

"We will beat the snot out of them," Skerrit said, warming to the thought of battle.

"At what cost?" Puck asked. "How many Seelie, vampires, humans, and witches will perish before the Black Queen is driven off?"

"Too many," Oberon agreed. "We will need a strategy that includes meeting the Black Queen on her world, or somewhere in between. First, a team must try and free Sionnach. He remains the most fearsome warrior of the Fae. With him, you may find the opportunity to kill the Black Queen. If not, having the four of you back with us will make us more powerful. It will also make her more rash."

"Enough for now," Titania said. "We need rest and time to consider the possibilities. In the morning I will meet with Morrigan, Cahal, and Skerrit to decide our course. If we are to be the tip of the spear, we should determine how best to strike. Puck will reach out to the Council of Four through Phiona. He will be able to best judge whether the others will join us to face an UnSeelie attack. My King, you can assemble the remaining Royals and begin developing your battle plans. One for here, without allies. One with allies. One if you should decide to invade Pandaemonium before they invade us, and one for somewhere in between."

Oberon smiled and said, "The Queen has spoken. Eat, drink, sleep. It may be your last time to relax for a long time to come."

Chapter 8

The familiar room made it more difficult to sleep. As a child he lived here until being sent to study in London with Bishop. The memories kept returning in short clips. Years jumbled, as he recalled striking aspects of being a half-human living in the world of the Fae. Five and discovering a horse that was a man that was both that was neither. Skerrit, in centaur configuration, towered above the boy. Any of his four hooves capable of squashing him. Not one moment of fear. He loved horses, even the hybrid Fae horses. To meet one he could talk to, and it talked back, was an unmeasurable thrill.

Older, learning not all Fae would treat you fairly. Tricked into going along with a gregarious Brownie to a lower kitchen to bake sweet bread. Brownies, in their brown pointed caps, and wrinkled skin, never talked much, but always smiled and often made faces at Cahal. Always in jest. In the kitchen, one rarely used, the Brownie became angry for no reason. He began to throw pots and pans. Turning on the young boy, he became thinner and his eyes burned with madness. The knife, taken from a utensil drawer, came toward him. Young, but a student of the Maerrighan, Cahal avoided the thrust, twisted the arm of the Fae until the weapon dropped, and then kicked the buttkis out of the short creature. Disarmed and over-matched, the Brownie ran crying from the kitchen.

This room brought back memories good and bad. He wanted sleep, but his mind fought back with visions not dreams.

He began the relaxation breathing techniques Bishop taught him. The moonstones, the magical pieces of round glass providing light, helped. As his breathing eased, and his body relaxed, the stones dimmed. The room became shadowed, as he came nearer to sleep.

At the edge of wake and slumber, he felt more than saw his door open and close. Through heavy eyelids he watched a ghost stand at the end of his bed. His breathing increased, the moonstones released a bit more illumination. The ghost became a woman dressed in white silk scarfs.

Her hands moved languidly. She pulled away a translucent section of cloth, baring her legs. The material floated to the floor. Her thighs white, firm, and looked silky soft.

The silken scarf covering her lower torso and hips unwrapped. Once around, twice around and the thin cover followed the first to the floor. Cale's eyes widened at the sight of her exposed lower body. Tight abs flowing into the v between her legs. Shaved or hair so fine it was invisible in the low light. Illumination increased as his heart rate rose.

The shawl around her shoulders fell away, followed by the cloth covering her chest. With the two pieces gone, only her head remained veiled. Her body was exquisite. A strange word for his mind to pull up. The perfect word for a perfect female body. Breasts not ponderous, but more than sufficient to keep someone entertained. Shoulders of soft white skin begged to be caressed. A waist so small he could easily touch fingers if he grasped her with both hands. Curves where curves belonged. Muscle where muscle looked delicious.

She moved in languid steps from the bottom to the side of the bed. His eyes locked upon her as she sat. Her body near enough, and the light high enough, to note her pubic hair was baby fine and white blonde. She pulled away the scarf-cap, exposing more white-blonde hair. It fell in curls, but did not reach her shoulders.

The face-veil came off last. Starting from the neck, she pulled it up. A neck worthy of soft nibbles and rushed kisses. A chin with a slight cleft and cupids'-bow lips of light pink. A barely-there smile revealed a tiny overbite of pearl white. The nose came to a little button tip. When the veil lifted, her eyes of dove-grey did not reflect light. Cool, intelligent eyes with a bit of haughtiness.

She leaned toward him, her breasts resting on his chest. She kissed him softly. Backed away, and returned with a more demanding kiss. His lips parted, and he accepted her tongue with his. The sweet taste of her mouth could not force his eyes closed. Her beauty extraordinary. He wanted to look at nothing but her. Certainly not the back of his own eyelids. Not when he could see this instead.

His hands reached around, finding the satin touch of her back more erotic for having a thin sheen of baby fuzz. She was solid and liquid and air and like nothing he ever felt before. He held a baby seal with the body of a Victoria Secrets model. The kiss seemed endless.

She slipped completely onto the bed, straddling him without allowing their lips to separate. His cock swollen and stiff beneath the thin blanket, inches away from finding her. As his desire grew, his chest ached from the drumming of his heart. Blood flowed into his penis and the moonstones grew ever brighter. The nearer he came to this woman, the more he wanted nothing so much as to enter her and remain forever.

Pulling her head away, fully aware of his desire, she pushed her boobs into his face, daring him to choose one. As one entered his mouth, nipple first, his hand cupped the other. Gently he massaged one and suckled the other until her hand found his penis through the cloth covering. Her squeeze made him squeeze her tit in return. His teeth closing on the other nipple. Nibble. Don't bite.

"Please, let me take this blanket off. Please, let me feel my body against yours."

He was not aware he spoke those wishes aloud until she said, "Of course you can take away this silly blanket. I'm here for you, Cahal. My body is yours. You can do anything you wish."

"Actually, he can't."

The beautiful, sexy, incredible body of white skin lifted off him. He watched as she flailed arms and wonderful legs, seeming to levitate before disappearing over the bedside. The thump he heard - her gorgeous ass landing on the hard, cold stone floor.

"Morgan?" he queried. He recognized her voice, and with the other woman no longer in his sight, he recognized the Maerrighan standing beside his bed. He sat up to see better. The woman he badly wanted to fuck came to her knees and rubbed her backside.

The dark-haired Fae warrior placed a palm on his chest and pushed him back.

"Get up and get out, Una," Morgan told the disheveled woman on the floor.

"You have no right, Morrigan," Una said, standing, breasts jutting forward.

"Your ass is currently bruised, Una," the Fae of nightmares whispered. "How would you like me to kick it naked into the corridor for everyone to see your lily-white skin with black and blue splotches?"

The beautiful woman walked around the taller, darker, deadlier woman, collected the scarves from the floor at the foot of the bed, blew Cale a kiss, and left, awkwardly wrapping silk and satin cloth around her exposed body.

"Would you like to explain any of that?" Cale asked.

"Una is Fin Bheara's wife," Morgan said. "She's considered, by some, to be the most beautiful Fairy alive. She is a child of nature, and able to seduce anything male by combining her shape, her beauty, her touch, and her scent. Once you lay eyes on her naked body, she controls you."

"I can attest to that," Cale admitted. "Why me?"

"I could stroke your ego and tell you how attractive you are to women, Fae and otherwise, but I do not think lust motivated Una. She wants to make Bheara jealous. He's a whore-hound who chases every woman he sees. His ego demands sexual conquests, in spite of being married to the most desirable female in the world. The other possibility is Bheara sent her to fuck you."

"Now I am confused. Why would he send his wife to have sex with me?"

"To challenge you to a duel of honor," Morgan replied. "Bheara is only jealous of power. He sees you as someone with the potential of becoming a force among the Folk. He envies your father for the same reason. Sionnach is the closest person to Oberon. He is my husband. And I have always refused Bheara's attempts to get me into his bed."

"A duel? Really?"

"If you had fucked Una he would have the legal right," she answered. "He is a great warrior, and one of our greatest swordsmen . . . and I'm not talking about his dick."

"I guess I should be happy you stopped her."

Morgan gave the young man a look someplace between pissed at his sarcasm and amused at his snark.

She went to the door, stepped outside, holding it open. A few seconds later she backed in, continuing to hold the door as a sprite flew through the narrow opening.

With his ardor cooled and his heart rate lowered, the light in the room retreated to the brightness of a three-quarter moon. More than enough to recognize one of the eight-inch tall winged nymphs from his youth.

"Morgan. Honestly?"

"Have fun," she responded, opening the door and leaving.

"Hello, Cahal," the sprite said, adding a giggle to the end of his name. "Long time no tease."

"Hello, Shaylee."

The Field Sprite settled on the bed between his knees. Cale recalled the randy dreams that haunted his change from boy to man, prior to being sent away. Shaylee often the cause and object of those fantasies.

Less than one-foot tall and built like the women one normally encounters in gaming videos. Always nude, Shaylee was a perfectly proportioned stunning example of a boy's lust. Large, round breasts with tiny dark red nipples and pink areola defied gravity. Her body curved into a slender waist before exploding into hips and buttocks. Her legs were perfect - feet at one end and pussy at the other. She posed to exploit the separation between her firm thighs, and displayed the tuft of brown fur that matched her short hair. Pixie cut, of course. With tissue thin wings spread across a frame of tiny bones, she could fly circles around the birds that shared the forests and fields.

Once she realized the effect she had on the young half-human, half-Fae, she lobbied to become his official message taker. Anytime anyone needed Cahal, Shaylee was asked to deliver the summons. With the glee of a child on a merry-go-round, she would float in front of his face, giggle her boobs, fly in circles and dive-bomb him from different directions, assuring he saw every inch of the eight-inch sprite. Message delivered, she gave him a face-full of her round rear, a little tush-push, and off she flew.

"Did Una get you excited and leave you without release?"

"It was a pleasant experience which ended rather abruptly," he answered. "Are you intending on teasing me into heart failure?"

"You mean because I am desirable, but too small to be of service?"

"I mean exactly that, as you well know. You enjoyed playing those games when I was a boy. I don't see why you would change now."

"Maybe because now you are a fully grown man," she replied. "I am small so I may fly. If I do not need to fly, I do not need to be small."

The gossamer wings began to retract. They disappeared as her body expanded. Within a few seconds, Shaylee lay atop him, at least five-feet-six and all of her measurements to scale.

"I feel your rod beneath me," she whispered, her face an inch away and her chest pressed against his. "I would like to see if I can handle such a large cock. What say you, Dúnmharú?"

Cahal did not answer. Instead he allowed his dark soul, his deep Fae to take control. The moonstones shone brightly as he lifted the sprite and placed her on her back. The blanket went sailing, and he buried his face between thighs he fantasized about for over a decade.

Overwhelmed by the force of his lust, Shaylee squeaked as his tongue worked against her lips, and his mouth sucked on the soft skin around her opening. His hands grabbed the round tits, fingers spread to grasp the melon-sized boobs and squeeze, eliciting another high-pitched squeak. A minute into licking and sucking the field nymph, one hand continued to kneed her breast, but the other began to finger her clit, moving in rhythm with his lips and tongue. Seeking the right places, the right rhythm. Finding both when her thighs locked over his head, and she attempted to bring her legs together while his head remained in the middle.

Shaylee's back arched. She reared up, a hip thrust that remained elevated with her buttocks muscles quivering. Cahal, instead of pressing harder, with more demand, reduced the tension, allowing his tongue and finger tips to play with her. The change brought on the orgasm, and the squeak turned to a drawn-out hum of intense pleasure. She came once - twice, and the third time rocked her so hard, she collapsed. Her breathing labored, her heart beating rapidly. The room lit as if by noon-day sunshine.

Giving the Fairy no time to think, recover, or reconsider, Cahal pushed the tip of his cock into her vagina. The width a bit much, but she was damp. It soon entered. As her vagina widened, so did her sea-blue eyes.

"I had no idea," she began, but the words stopped as he pushed his length into the woman beneath him. His mouth covered hers, greedily searching for her tongue as his hips began the push and release of a deep, demanding fuck.

More sprite magic, or perhaps female lust. Her vagina accepted him, and she began to match his thrusts with her own. Later, Cahal decided he discovered the origin of the phrase 'banging.' The combination of the two lovers thrusting, gyrating, and demanding each other caused the heavy bed to bounce on the stone floor. The feet banging, and the sound echoing off the four walls.

This time Shaylee screamed when the orgasm wracked her, and he joined her with his own release and matching scream.

He lay atop her, enjoying the feel of her luscious body beneath him. Both of them covered in a sheen of perspiration, making the connection more tactile. She smelled of pasture flowers, hay, and animal.

"I am glad I teased you as a boy," she whispered. Her breath tickled his ear. "It was worth the wait for you to become a man."

"Shaylee, I'm going to pull out," he whispered.

"Oh, no."

"Then roll you onto your stomach and start again," he added.

"Oh, yea."

Chapter 9

The unfamiliar room made it difficult for her to concentrate. Annabeth rarely woke comfortably. Rising in an unfamiliar place made her more uncomfortable. Waking and realizing the position she had accepted, and the speed required to get her into place only added to her doubts. Morgan calling in Cale's favor and taking him left her without a strong pillar. Others believed she could pull this off. She wished she had their confidence.

From the bed she could see everything in the efficiency apartment. Two doors: one to the outside; the key on the desk. One to a bathroom; she guessed. The closet was open, prepared with hangars. Her clothes remained in her bags. The outfit she wore to Atlanta lay on the floor. The kitchenette included a full-size stainless-steel refrigerator.

Curious, and a bit hopeful, she slipped off the bed, let the thin blanket fall away from her naked body, and checked the fridge. Someone made sure sealed packets of blood occupied a shelf. She took one, placed it in the counter-top microwave for fourteen-seconds, and removed the warm liquid. She bit off the tip of the straw-like funnel at one corner, and smelled the aroma of warm, nearly fresh plasma. More than enough to finish waking her, and sufficient to get her through at least one day.

Her phone chimed. Michele Quan.

"Glad to see you made it," she said, answering the FaceTime call.

"Rested and ready. We're at the airport, but didn't want to make the trip in until you were up," the security expert said.

"We?"

"Maggie and Simone flew down from Quebec." A loud bark startled Quan and the vampire. "Sorry. Daegen came with them. He says hello."

It was not the same as having Cale near, but knowing she had friends and help elicited a smile.

"Simone?"

"The Maerrighan called her. Asked if she could provide support since she borrowed Cale. Simone decided to come herself," Quan explained. "You ready for visitors?"

"I will be by the time you get here," she answered. "Bring anything Jace's people didn't load," she added.

"Will do," and the call ended.

The cell buzzed. A call not a video.

"You monitoring my calls?" she asked Burrell.

"We monitor signals," he told her. "We don't listen. I didn't want to disturb you, but once I knew you had spoken to Ms. Quan, I decided to check in. If you haven't discovered it yet, there are blood packs in the fridge."

"Found 'em."

"Not perfect, but better than trying to hunt in an unfamiliar location, and less time consuming," he said. "Arina's coterie has been busy while we slept. We need to meet soon."

"Michele and friends are inbound," she replied. "Have them taken somewhere we can meet, and send someone to take me to them. After I shower and dress."

"Twenty-minutes," he said. "That enough time?"

"Yep."

Tom Farway collected Annabeth and delivered her to a third-floor parlor which had been converted into a communications and conference center. He spent a major part of the day becoming familiar with the plantation manor's layout. Annabeth did not bother asking if he was acting as a bodyguard at Bishop's request. She knew the answer, and better to not place the Council pilot-employee in a position where his presence might be considered overstepping.

Michele and Simone greeted her with hugs, after Dae bounced off her legs and received a neck scratch. Maggie waved from across the room. She was seated at a table with a half-dozen HD monitor screens and an array of track pads, keyboards, and electronic pens. Jace, dressed in a three-piece dark blue suit, sat beside the techie, but turned away from the electronic equipment. Farway followed her. He knew Michele and Maggie, and was introduced to Simone, Jace, and Daegen.

The Overlord of Southeastern North America, from the Carolinas to the Yucatan, appraised her crew. Jace Burrell and Simone Sinclair looked like a high society power couple. Simone's silk blouse, business skirt, and low-heel sandals went well with his suit and tie. Maggie wore a long-sleeve striped shirt over a t-shirt. Jeans and hiking boots. Michele wore tactical black. Form-fitted lycra more than accentuated her chest, but also stayed out of the way in a fight. The combat pants did not have multiple pockets so they fit snuggly, and were tucked into low-heel black boots. Tom still wore his pilot's uniform, more wrinkled and less crisp than when they landed. For her part, she wore a short-sleeve sweater pull-over, skinny jeans, and ankle boots.

They certainly did not look like a force to be reckoned with. They did present a formidable blend of strength, knowledge, experience, and expertise.

"You said Arina's coterie had been busy," she said to Burrell. "What's up?"

"Peachtree District Mall is an upscale business and shopping center on Peachtree Avenue. It's located two blocks from the Capital. Lots of glass and marble. Covers a couple of acres and three levels. Five-Star restaurant, business offices for a law firm, world-renown architect, an internet app developer, and a combination Pilates-Barre-Fitness studio for women-only. Wealthy women. Restaurant and a half-dozen shops on the first level. Middle level is completely made up of shops. High-end clothiers, specialty foods, antique, jewelry, and such. The top level is where the business offices and the fitness studio are located."

"Sounds like an expensive place to visit," the younger vampire said.

"At four p.m. an estimated one-hundred thralls and human servants took control. They tossed the unarmed security personnel out, and locked off elevators and stairwells to the underground parking facilities. The mall has two double-door entrances on Peachtree, an entrance at the end of each side, bottom floor. The rear is a service alley with two service doors and four garage-style doors for the loading bay. Anything coming in comes through the underground or through the rear bays. Service elevators are on each end. Two escalators and a glass-elevator inside for people. Stairwell access to the roof. Single roof access."

"The people inside?"

"All entrance-exit points have been locked, barricaded, and covered by armed guards," he answered. "Other than the security personnel ejected, they have not let anyone else leave."

"We have video," Maggie announced. Everyone moved to stand behind her. When she noticed, she told them, "No need to gang up. Arina spent some serious dinero on this system." The video on her screen repeated across several monitors.

"The first shot is from a police cameraman stationed across the street in front of the mall," she said.

"You hacked the Atlanta PD?" Annabeth asked.

"Yep. The restaurant on the first floor has windows along the front and side wall. It would make it vulnerable for a smash and enter. The bad guys have placed civilians on the floor and in chairs in front of the windows. If the Bobbies try to blow through or use an armored vehicle to break in, they will take out a lot of innocents."

"The restaurant was busy that early?" Farway asked.

"Happy hour and five-star early-bird specials," Maggie answered. "From their social media accounts, they attract a decent number of politicians and business people ditching work early."

"What about the other potential entry points?" Michele asked.

"I can give you three-sixty from a variety of security cameras, plus the local television news vans. Every entry-exit appears barricaded. The front double-doors also have satchels tied where they can be seen."

"Satchels. Bombs?" Quan asked.

"Bombs or decoys to make the police think twice before trying to make a forced entry," Maggie replied.

"They will be real explosives," Burrell said. "Arina would not have wasted time with a bluff. I doubt her lieutenants will do anything less."

"Anyone want to see inside?" the techie asked.

"You can see inside the mall?" Burrell asked, moving forward for the first time.

"The security office is mainly a kiosk at the entrance. Basic CCTV with cheap monitors. Somebody enjoyed visiting porn sites on the clock and left the connection open. For a high-end sophisticated shopping center, they went cheap on electronics. The cameras don't give a lot of definition, but you can tell what's what."

Maggie began scrolling through a series of cameras. They could see the first level, shops closed. Second level, the same.

"A Chick-fil-A," Farway said. "This caters-to-the-rich mall has a Chick-fil-A."

"You're in Atlanta," Burrell said. "And the employees need a place for lunch."

There was more activity on the top level. The doors leading to the law firm had people in dark clothing with guns milling outside. The double-doors leading into the architectural offices were open. People moved about beyond the receptionist's desk. Two people, once more dressed in dark clothing, stood outside the fitness studio.

"AK-47s," Quan said. "Sidearms, too."

"I connected a facial app and bean counter to the video streaming into my laptop," Maggie told them. "The software recognized some from Council file-photos. Others were classified as Bad Guys based on location, clothing, and whether they are armed. Counter is up to thirty-seven total. I haven't been able to access any cameras inside the law offices, the architect's place, or the fitness studio. I'm pretty sure I have all the bogeys mapped in the corridors and the restaurant."

"We estimate twice that number for our plans," Michele said.

"There's more bad news," Maggie said. "I ran building security tapes back. I found this happening on the loading dock following the initial assault."

They watched a truck back up to the ramp. Men and women in dark clothes, lifted the back door and began wheeling boxes out. Boxes about the size of coffins.

"I counted five," Burrell said. "Arina's vampires are inside the mall waiting for the sun to go down."

"Keep watching," Maggie warned.

A second truck took the place of the first one. Once more coffin-sized crates were wheeled off and into the mall's cargo bay.

"Eight more," Burrell said. "It doesn't add up. I know of the five renegades, and I know where the other terrestrial vampires she turned are located. I have watchers on each of them."

"Five she turned with permission," Annabeth said. "What if she turned some of her thralls without the Vampire Directorate's permission?"

"She can't," he answered. "Part of seeking permission is the fact only the original non-terrestrials know the method to complete the final turn. If a vampire tries to turn a thrall without the last step, they end up with a blood-crazed mindless dhampir."

"Or eight of them," Maggie said. "What happens if they set them loose?"

"Vampire zombies with an insatiable need for fresh blood. Creatures of immense strength and speed, and without a sense of self. They will ignore pain. They will feel nothing physically or emotionally. What do you think they will do?" Burrell asked.

"Show the world their greatest fears regarding blood-sucking, soulless, supernatural monsters," Maggie said. She slowly turned away from her computers, her eyes bounced between Annabeth and Burrell, and she finally said, "Sorry. I wasn't describing you guys."

"Doesn't mean you didn't nail it," Annabeth said. "If they let those dhampirs loose, there is no telling how much damage they will do to people in the mall, and to vampires everywhere when the news media release their pictures."

"It's after sundown," Michele said, interrupting the thoughts of non-sentient vampires. "Have you picked up any of Arina's lieutenants?"

"None I could swear to," the seated blonde replied, glad for the change of subject - sort of. "But the service lifts could have taken them anywhere. They could be in a closed store, or in one or all of the offices on the top level."

"You may wish to listen to this," Simone said. She was standing in front of a television, and not one with CCTV video streaming. "Local news station."

Everyone listened as a reporter told of a conversation he had with one of the 'terrorists' inside the Peachtree District Mall.

"The person who called me finished by claiming to have vampires inside the center. I quote that person now. Vampires prepared to feed on the humans. She also said they expected Arina Kishka's return to Atlanta within thirty-hours. If the most powerful vampire in the United States was not inside the mall by midnight tomorrow, they would begin killing hostages. If Kishka was not delivered by four a.m., they would release a hoard of wild vampires, and join them in a rampage against the people of Atlanta. The woman said they consist of humans, thralls, and vampires and they would continue to hunt and kill, day and night. She promised they would move out from Atlanta, into Georgia, the Southeast, and beyond."

The reporter began speaking about the relationship between the three races and the failure by authorities to properly segregate and monitor vampires, Fae, and witches. It did not matter witches were technically human. Simone muted him.

"They have already gone public," she said. "They must be stopped, and they must be prevented from harming a single human. If not, the outcry by people fed the images of out-of-control and overly powerful non-humans by the media elitists will fuel a movement to gather and tag vampires, Fae, and not-technically-human witches." The refined French-born aristocrat spat those final words.

"And you must do it without me, Annabeth," Burrell said.

This pronouncement brought everyone in the room to quiescence. A gunshot would not have brought the attention to him his simple statement created.

"You are one of five non-terrestrial vampires," Annabeth said. "An Exemplar. The most ancient of the vampires. The most powerful. You are an army, possibly invulnerable, and probably immortal. You are Ssara Den. Why would you not help stop this stupidity?"

"Because of everything you just said," he replied. "If I am seen as the one who stops them, what are you? Certainly not the Overlord of the territory. For those members of Arina's coterie who survive, and those who would prefer not being there in the first place, they must see you as their lord. Not me. They already fear and respect me. If the others who are not here, but who watch see you take control and stop this, as you say, stupidity, you will become their regent."

"And if I fail?" she asked.

"Then I am the fallback," he answered. "For you to fail will mean you are truly dead, and it will no longer matter if I steal your thunder. It will, however, make it more difficult for me to pasteurize these territories."

"Pasteurize," Michele asked.

"If Annabeth cannot assume the mantle of Overlord, and I am faced with putting down this insurrection. I will also be forced to eliminate every vampire, thrall, servant, and hanger-on from here to Central America. Not only because I will be unable to trust any of them, but to show the world we police our own."

"You're talking about thousands," Maggie said. "I've run the numbers, Thousands."

"I would prefer not doing it," he said to them. "Annabeth must be the one who ends this. Preferably with as few humans killed as possible. I have already named her as my Overlord. If you want those thousands to survive, and for this event to become old news within the week, I suggest the rest of you do everything you can to support her."

"You're seriously not going to help?" Farway asked.

"My plane is waiting to take me back to Vancouver," he said. "My car is waiting in the garage. This was how it had to be, regardless of this act of bravado to free Arina. I have placed my Overlord in her position. I must now move aside and see if she is the vampire Bishop believes her to be."

With nothing more to say, Jace Burrell, nee Ssara Den, left the room, and left the mess with Annabeth and her haphazard team.

"I would have done the same thing," Simone said. "It doesn't make sense, but it is how leaders are made. The fire will turn cold metal into hard steel, or melt it into useless sludge."

Annabeth turned to Maggie and ordered, "Everything you can find on the mall and everyone inside. Everyone, Maggie. Hack, steal, or go there yourself if you must, but I want diagrams, plans, numbers, players, and positions and I want everything in one hour."

Maggie actually saluted before she began making a flurry of keystrokes.

"Michele, get our armory together. Find out if any of Burrell's rent-a-cops have military training, and if they can be bought. Once you have a number, decide how best to assign weapons and targets."

She turned to Tom Farway. "Get Kristy and the other two pilots here. I know enough about Council pilots to know you have military training. I need soldiers. You were a leatherneck?"

"We prefer being called Royals," he replied.

"Then get your Royal arse to work and find us a way inside," she ordered.

"Yes, ma'am," he replied, without sarcasm. "What about Sinclair's pilots?"

"They aren't combat qualified," Simone answered. Which leaves the dog and me."

"Dae will stay here and bite anyone who tries to interrupt the work. Right Dae?"

The shepherd may or may not have understood the words, but he understood his job. He lay by the door with ears up and eyes open.

"Simone, I need you to come with me. I need something special, and you are the only one who can do it."

"Wonder what she needs," Tom said after the two women departed.

Dae gave a low growl. A soft, not-exactly-menacing rumble.

"Okay. I was only wondering," he told the dog. "Maggie, can you give me a screen with schematics for the mall?"

Chapter 10

Morgan entered Cahal's room after daybreak. She stood in darkness and waited for the moonstones to recognize her presence and increase the light. The Fae considered to have no sense of humor nearly burst into girlish giggles at the sight of Cahal and Shaylee tangled in legs, arms, and bed sheets. She had no idea of what positions the two managed the night before, but how they could possibly sleep in their current arrangement escaped her.

She began to unravel the puzzle, extricating Cahal from the fairy one limb at a time. The part-Fae, part-human (with his heritage revealed, he could no longer be considered half-and-half) did not waken. Shaylee remained comatose as well, though she did produce a sound between a groan and a moan as Morgan lifted the man up and away from the bed.

"Sex drunk," the Royal said, shaking her head as she carried the two-hundred-pound body as if she carried a young child.

The King's Castle was ancient, filled with magic, like the moonstones, and antiques, like the round table. Walls four-feet thick of quarried granite and imported marble tiles for floors. It was also modern. Wired for electricity, fiber optic cables for electronics, satellite receivers to stay in touch with the world, and plumbing.

The Maerrighan placed the fairy-intoxicated not-so-Dúnmharú-at-the-moment on the floor on a marbled shower with floating glass door and a number of shower heads designed to direct spray at various levels. She pointed every nozzle at the curled form, made sure the digital thermometer setting hovered between iceberg and frozen tundra, and turned them on.

The scream came and was immediately choked off by his jaw clenching. Fully awake, if not fully functional, he scrambled to a corner in an attempt to avoid some of the icy spray.

Shaylee, roused by the yelp flew into the bathroom, back to her normal height. She found the Maerrighan with a hand covering her mouth and tears in her eyes. Cahal sat naked on the floor of the shower, backed into a corner. Shivering.

"If I had known it could get that tiny," she said, eyes on his crotch, "I could have remained this size."

Unable to contain herself, Morgan laughed until her sides hurt. A sound not heard in the lands of Fae Folk in eons.

"I know now why your title is Nightmare," Cahal said, walking beside Morgan, matching her stride.

"Perhaps you have learned a lesson," she said. "Sex with a Fae, especially a nymph, can be overwhelming. Had it been Una and not Shaylee, it might have been Fin Bheara who woke you instead of me. A cold blade would be more chilling than a cold shower."

"I should thank you for saving my life by trying to kill me with sex?"

"Cahal Kearney, had I wanted to kill you with sex I would not have brought a field nymph to your bed. I would have done it my-self."

The hesitation in his step allowed Morgan to move ahead. He could not see if she appeared serious. He caught up quickly and asked, "What's the plan?"

"We're going to Titania's private chamber to meet with her and Skerrit," she said.

The pair continued in silence to the far side of the castle. The Maerrighan did not bother to knock. They entered a spacious stu-dio with floor to ceiling windows twelve-feet high. They provided a panoramic view of the sun rising above the Fae village and the pasture beyond the village.

Skerrit, dressed in fawn-colored leathers, sat on a small sofa. Holding him it became a small chair beneath a huge butt. His wild red hair pulled back and tied into a ponytail. His equally wild red beard braided into two lengthy rows adorned with black beads.

Titania, also dressed in leathers, leaned against the front of her desk. Arms crossed, and feet crossed at the ankles, she ap-peared to be in deep thought, looking up from the floor as the newcomers arrived.

The Queen's leathers looked worn and supple. Practical and comfortable. The blood-red color of her buttoned tunic matching the tight britches. Her shirt, untucked, was only fastened by a single button half-way down. Titania, always modestly dressed in Cahal's memories, looked like she could model expensive lingerie for a lot of money. Her feet were bare.

She noticed Cahal's attempt not to stare. "In my quarters I prefer to be comfortable, Cahal. It also helps me think more clearly."

"Makes me think, too," Skerrit quipped. "Only not about what I'm needin' to think about."

"Males," the Queen murmured. Morgan gave Cahal a slant-eyed glance, agreeing with her liege without a word.

Titania buttoned two additional holes.

For the first time, seeing Titania and Skerrit in leathers, Cahal realized Morgan wore her own battle leathers. A black suede shirt under a reinforced black leather corset. Skin tight pants of matte black tucked into thigh-high boots, laced from ankles to thighs with flat leather thongs. She did not wear her gloves, forearm greaves, or the sword belt with filigree silver runes, otherwise she was prepared for a fight.

"If I have to wear leather, do I get to pick the color?" he asked.

"Leathers are for dominant alphas," Skerrit said. "You haven't been out of wool knee-britches that long. Sheep's skin might be a better choice."

"Enough," Titania ordered. "I know you enjoy your banter, but we have a serious task ahead. You wear whatever you prefer when you fight for your life, Cahal. We have worn and trusted our leathers for many ages and too many struggles to change now, regardless of the advances in combat clothing humans have developed."

"I meant no disrespect," Cahal said.

"Noted," the Queen replied. "Morrigan, you have spent the most time with Oberon since his return. Where do we begin?"

"The path from Earth to Pandaemonium will require eighteen portal changes. Most are rather simple, but two may require fighting indigenous species. If the paths are clear, we can plane-travel there in twelve-hours."

"We?" Cahal asked. "You aren't a hybrid."

"I, and a few select Fae will travel with you until the final gate before Pandaemonium," she replied. "We can help if trouble occurs between entry and exit portals. We can also cover your retreat."

"Titania, Cahal, and I go into the Black Queens realm alone," Skerrit said. "The hope is no alarms are set off because of our mixed blood. We will be careful about Fae magik. Using more than our natural abilities could attract more attention than we are prepared to deal with. We do not spook the locals, and we locate the place Sionnach is being held. We free him, and make our way to the exit."

"Don't forget," Morgan said, "you are to attempt to assassinate Caileach."

The name the Maerrighan uttered came out as Kî lax.

"Who is . . ."

"**DONOSAYIT!**" Skerrit jumped from his chair to stop Cahal from saying the name. "That Morrigan did is bad enough. We do not ever say her true name. She is The Black Queen. Queen of Air and Darkness. The Unspoken Evil. You all know the power held in a name. What if she could appear with a single calling, not said three times?"

"Relax, Skerrit," The black-clad female said. "I will not say her name again. Nor will Cahal. Right?"

"Won't say it, but shouldn't I know more about her if we plan on assassinating her?" he asked.

"She is cunning, cruel, and merciless," Titania said. "She is beautiful, brilliant, and insane. She created the magic that allows Fae the ability to produce glamours used to conceal our true appearance. She hates the light, prefers living in the shadows, and commands any creature with a foul soul."

"How will I recognize her?" he asked.

"Look on Morrigan," Titania told him. "They are twin sisters."

Cahal sat cross-legged on his bed. Someone had cleaned the room and made the bed while he was in the meeting. He wondered if the silk sheets were salvageable after the night with

Shaylee. Morgan sat in the same position, facing him. They had returned here after the short strategy session.

"Not a lot of detail for our strategic assault and rescue mission," he said.

"Battle plans will be made by Oberon," she responded. "What you and the others must do will require quick thinking and decisions made as events unveil themselves. To go into Pandaemonium with a detailed plan of action would be a waste of time."

"If we come up against the Black Queen, can we kill her?"

"I do not know," Morgan admitted. "I have not seen my sister in one-hundred-thousand-years. What she may have evolved into, I cannot guess. She was one of the most powerful Fae Royals. I imagine her banishment has provided time and motivation for her to increase her skills."

"Why was she banished?"

"I will give you the short version," the black-clad, dark eyed woman said. "She was betrothed to Oberon. It was a match everyone thought perfect. That she loved him was undeniable. When the passage to Earth was discovered, this planet was home to the first civilizations. A race of unimaginable strength. Brilliant minds. They were the Titans. Another race invaded Earth, coming through a plane-gate with weapons of devastation. The myths of the Greek gods and goddesses come from these invaders. The battle between the Titans and the Olympians proved costly to both sides. It ended with a shaky truce."

Morgan uncurled and turned to sit on the side of the bed, facing a blank stone wall. "When Oberon crossed the plane, he met Titania, the princess-daughter of the last Titan king and an Olympian goddess. There were no others left for Titania to mate with. No way to continue the race. The Olympians had fallen into debauchery and sloth by then as well. Humans only beginning to find their footing as the new shepherds of the planet."

She lost herself in the cut stones of the wall, remembering a far-away time. Following a moment of reflection, she continued.

"Oberon fell in love with Titania. You see her, Cahal. You have been around her enough to recognize her strength of character, her quick mind, her fearlessness. Her beauty. When he told my sister she would not become Queen, she became enraged. In her madness she attempted to kill Titania."

"Oberon stopped her?" he asked.

"I stopped her," Morgan answered. "Oberon took her from me with the intent of killing her for what she tried to do. But he still had feelings for her. He blamed himself for her madness, and banished her instead. He took her far away, making sure she was unaware of the plane-passages he used. He left her on a distant world in another dimension. He left her alone."

"She's not alone anymore," Cahal said.

"No. Plane-travelers have spread tales of the Black Queen for millennia. Stories of a powerful sorceress who created a world of cruel, dangerous creatures. The more Oberon heard, the more he believed it to be his intended wife building an UnSeelie hoard. He was right."

"Morgan, do you want to tell me about my father and mother now?" he asked.

"Until your arrival in this castle, my name among equals was, and still is, Morrigan. I have many titles, from Crow to Nightmare. My husband had an affair with a human, the daughter of a Legacy Witch. When your mother died, I did not rejoice, but I did not mourn. Bishop brought you to live with the Fae when you were only three-years old."

"I kind-of remember," he said. "I remember when I met you. I was unable to say Morrigan."

"I hated you up to the moment when you stood in front of me, grabbed my fingers in your tiny hand, and called me Morgan," she said. "I was bathed in the heat of anger. The other Fae were prepared to intervene before I swept you to the land of the dead." She turned to face him. "You squeezed my fingers and said, Morgan again. You smiled at me, and my heart broke. All I saw was your father. All I could think of was him asking me to look out for Damiana and his unborn twins while he went with Oberon in search of my sister. I failed your mother and your sister, Cahal. I failed Sionnach. Morrigan failed. But Morgan would not fail caring for this child. For you."

"And you never have," he said.

"You owe me a favor, Dúnmharú," she said. Her demeanor the cold, emotionless side that proved the Maerrighan always ruled this woman's spirit. "I failed you by calling in your payment. I have sent you on a path that will place you before the Black Queen, in a world of unspeakable evil creatures. In my haste to do something for Sionnach, I placed his only son on a course with death."

"I would have chosen to go without owing for a favor," Cahal told her. "I am Dúnmharú, Morgan. It is the Black Queen who started down a path that will end with me. The Executioner."

London. Soho. Cahal. Age 12.

Cahal sat in the backseat of the rented Ford sedan. Morgan sat to his left, the Fae Royal dressed in a grey pantsuit with high neck midnight black blouse. She wore ankle boots and carried a designer clutch instead of a sword.

"This is not your first time among humans, Cahal," she said. "You have been to schools in the United States, Italy, and Egypt. You have taken lessons in Ireland, Scotland, and Russia."

"I always knew when my time was done I would return home," he said. "This is different. I don't know if I will ever go back."

"Course you will, nephew," Puck said from behind the driver's wheel. Glamoured as Robin Goodfellow, the Fae looked like a jolly banker. His red hair and beard smoothed. Wearing a navy pin-striped three-piece suit complete with gold watch fob protruding from the vest pocket. "The enclave in Tipperary has been there ages and will be there waiting for your return."

"How long will that be?"

Neither Fae spoke. Cahal's time with Bishop would be up to the vampire. The three-story stone and brick house would be his home for an untold time. Time needed for the youth to grow into the Dúnmharú. Or not. If Cahal could not master the requirements, then another life awaited the human-Fae hybrid.

The sun already set behind the homes and the turrets, towers, and skyscrapers behind the Soho district. Electric lights designed to look like old gas lanterns from the eighteen-hundreds lit the sidewalk. Puck exited on the street side, careful not to open his door onto traffic. He popped the boot of the Ford, extracting two leather suitcases. Cahal had a satchel between his feet, resting on the floorboard. The three bags held all he brought.

"Knives?" Morgan asked.

"At my feet," he answered.

"Short sword?"

"In the longer suitcase."

"Shuriken?"

"Feet."

"Garrote?"

"Bag."

"Then you are ready to live among humans," the Queen of Nightmares said.

Taking the pronouncement as Morgan's way of saying good-bye, Cahal Kearney stepped onto the sidewalk in London's West End for the first time.

The door at the top of the steps opened. The interior lights framing a young woman dressed in a gossamer top and the short-est mini-dress imaginable. Black mesh stockings ended in black knee boots with three-inch heels. The side lights on the portico lit flame-red hair allowed to fly loose and long. She slipped a small bag over her right shoulder, and skipped down the steps as if they were not there.

She stopped at the bottom to appraise the boy standing beside the car. The boy with his mouth open, enthralled by the teenage beauty with the deepest emerald colored eyes he had ever seen.

"Hello, Puck," she said to Goodfellow, giving the Fae a finger wave. "You must be Kearney," she said, bending forward to place her head even with Cahal's. This near he noticed the fangs as she smiled, and could not help noticing her cleavage. "Guess we'll meet officially later," she said. "Tonight I have plans. All of London waiting." She stroked his cheek with her fingers and melted into the shadows between streetlights.

"Breath, Cahal," Puck said. He stood beside the boy, suitcases in hands. "Unlike Miss Annabeth Hughes, you aren't a vampire. You need air."

"Annabeth Hughes?" he asked.

"Bishop's ward," Puck answered. "She lives here."

Cahal followed Puck up the steps, giving the front of the building a thorough examination. If he was going to live here and Annabeth Hughes lived here, this may not be such a bad place to stay for a while.

On the landing Puck passed the luggage to a black man the same height as the Fae.

"This is Dikembe Kadi, Bishop's butler, gatekeeper, and bodyguard," Puke introduced the stolid man in the dark uniform of a butler. "Formerly Sergeant Kadi of the Congolese Army, so tread softly Cahal. There is more to Master Dikembe than meets the eye."

"Follow me. I will show you your room," Kadi said. His accent London English with a strong hint of French.

Puck hugged the boy, pulled away, and turned him to the doorway.

Cahal closed the door, not bothering to watch Puck and Morgan drive away.

Chapter 11

Michele Quan made the decision. With Arina's ex-coterie of humans, thralls, and terrestrial-vampires dressed in varying degrees of goth to present the best vampiric horror appearance for television, they would wear grays. The color would allow them to blend into shadowy spaces, and they would recognize friend from foe during the frenzy of fight.

A call to four military surplus retailers, an American Express card, and a bonus for quick delivery resulted in four vans arriving within an hour with the requested clothing and accessories. Since nothing deemed a weapon was purchased, the transactions were not subject to any delays for background checks.

Kristy Nichol had joined them, along with the two pilots who ferried Michele across the pond. James McWaters, former RAF, and Harry Campbell, Royal Navy Fleet Air Arm helicopter pilot, though licensed to fly anything with wings. Both trained in single combat as part of evade and escape programs.

Quan hired four of the security agents away from the agency contracted by Burrell. Ex-military with combat experience in the Middle East.

The dirty dozen. Twelve against two-hundred. Thirteen if you count Daegen.

Maggie would remain at the house. It offered all of the electronics she required in one place and communications with the team members would be no issue.

Simone walked into the room, noticed the uniform appearance and the relatively poor fit for most, and said, pointedly, "I think not," when Michele held up a grey combination in a size she guessed might fit the witch.

Annabeth followed three minutes later. Sound stopped.

Her flame-red hair was pulled back. Artfully applied make-up concealed her freckles, lengthened her face, and made her green eyes deeper, more serious. She wore a garnet-colored Indian style tunic with a square neck. Not a casual look, as she had diamond earrings, and a diamond pendant on a platinum-gold necklace. Beneath the tunic she wore black silk slacks with flared cuffs.

Christian Louboutin slip-on shoes with low-heels completed the look.

"You look older," Maggie said.

"You look serious," Tom added.

"You don't look ready for a fight," Michele said.

"Tom, did you find another way into the mall?" she asked, taking charge and ignoring the comments.

"Basement," Farway answered. He went to the console he had used to scan diagram and pulled up three-dimensional schematics. "Most of downtown Atlanta has underground access. There's a complete shopping area located beneath the streets. The Peachtree District Mall has its own single level of underground parking."

"Which has been closed off by the bad guys," Michele said.

"But it does not run under the entire length of the mall," he continued. "At the North end a section of the basement from the previous building, a sugar depot, was not used. It's blocked off to the garage, but there is an access tunnel for maintenance that connects to the first floor. It's linked to the mall's engineering section."

"Which get us from the basement to the first level," Annabeth said. "How do we get to the basement?"

"On the other side of the street which connects to Peachtree, across from where the old sugar depot sat, is the equally old Deluxe Hotel. Caters to politicians, lobbyists, and such, he said. The basement bar is rather famous. It was a private club during prohibition. Known as a place that made its own alcoholic concoctions."

"Thanks for the cultural tour," a security guard said. "How does this help?"

"They would need sugar for distilling," Annabeth said. "They would not want to be seen hauling in bags of sugar, so, a tunnel?"

"I found a pre-1925 diagram of underground access tunnels, sewers, shafts, and such," Tom answered. "It shows a tunnel between the two basements. One not showing up on later plans."

"It could have been sealed," the same guard said.

"Or people paid off to forget about it," Maggie chimed in.

"If it isn't there, any other ways in?" Annabeth asked Tom.

"Only what we know about. Any of those would require a hard entrance."

"Michele, is one of those uniforms for me?"

"I guessed at the size, Annabeth" the Eurasian replied. "I'm pretty sure I got it right."

"We'll leave in multiple cars," the new Overlord of the Southeastern Territories said. "I'm going to the front of the mall. I need to speak with the law enforcement officers, and then I intend to give Arina's lieutenants the opportunity to surrender."

"You planning on walking up to the front door?" Campbell asked. "Seems a bloody risk not worth the taking."

"While everyone's attention is on me, the rest of you will enter the Deluxe, and get to the bar in the basement. One of our new security agents will maintain watch. Make sure no one else follows you in, and no one leaves. Simone will use her magic to locate a shaft, if there is one."

The redhead looked to the electronic expert, and asked, "Do you have everything you need?"

"More than enough," Maggie replied. "Arina might have hated humans for the advances in technology, but it didn't stop her from loading up and the latest, greatest equipment."

"If a shaft is located, they tell you, and you tell me," Annabeth said and Maggie nodded.

"I will keep the vampires inside the mall talking. I imagine their subservients will be interested and paying attention. It should provide the time to get through and make your way up onto the first level. Leave another guard to cover the basement."

"That only leaves eight," the ex-Marine who had spoken earlier. Toole was his name.

"Most insertion teams are smaller," another ex-guard said. "Camila Raoul, ex-Army Ranger," she said as introduction to her new boss.

"Few women graduated Ranger certification," Tom Farway said.

"Only the best," Raoul replied. The smile she added a thin one. "Men don't like getting shown up by a shortie, no matter what they might say out loud. I got tired of the comments and left."

"I can't say I have experienced the problems you faced, Ms. Raoul. The tall, asian-looking woman with the large automatic pistol strapped to her thigh is Michele Quan. She runs security for me, and she does not take shit from anyone. She also does not give a damn if someone is male, female, human, vampire, or Fae. Follow orders, protect your teammates, and come home alive is all she demands. Can you follow her?"

"Yes, ma'am," the ex-Ranger said.

"The rest of you?" she queried the room.

A chorus of agreement followed.

"When Maggie tells me you are inside, I walk away from the mall entrance," Annabeth said. "Anyone with any authority will move back up to the third level to discuss their options. Simone will use her magic to mask you and fog the first level. I expect the seven of you, in whatever method and means Ms. Quan decides, will clear the first level, especially the restaurant."

"There will be a lot of noise," Toole said.

"No, there will not," Simone responded. "I control the air, and I control what travels through the air, including sounds. Anything short of a bomb exploding on the first level will not be heard on the upper levels, or outside of the mall."

"By the time I change and join you, I expect the hostages to be freed. We will leave two guards to protect them, and then we move to the second level," Annabeth told them.

"Why not send the hostages out?" Raoul asked.

"Television," Maggie answered. "The bad guys will see them."

"Just so," Annabeth said. "Maggie, I believe Jace sent his driver back after he flew off. Please tell him to have the car ready. Daegen and I will meet him in five minutes."

At his name, the black shepherd lifted his head, ears up.

"You heard right, Dae," she said. "You're with me. I may need you to find the others in Simone's fog, and I trust you covering my back."

In response, a wag of a long, thick tail and a doggie happy look.

Annabeth turned and left, her black shadow a step behind.

Maggie distributed ear-plug communications receivers. The tiny inserts included a   micro-microphone for an all-in-one system.

"No turning them on and off," she said. "I control who hears what and when. I'll make sure team members are linked in at the proper time." As she handed Simone the flesh-colored plug, she said, "The special help Annabeth needed you for. The make-up and outfit?"

Simone smiled.

"Nice work," the tech said. "Took a teenager and brought back a bad-ass who looks like a million-bucks."

"She has always been a bad-ass," the French-Canadian witch replied. "I made her look like a million-dollars, and it wasn't actually too difficult."

"Maybe I can get some help before my next date," Maggie quipped.

"That might be a lot more difficult," Simone replied, moving away before Maggie could decide if she had been dissed or joked with.

Chapter 12

Annabeth's first hurdle required getting through the throng of curious citizens and anxious reporters kept away from the action by police barricades.

Burrell's driver proved his worth by moving the oversized Land Rover Range Rover SVAutobiography through the congested streets. The gunmetal gray SUV with dark-tinted windows looked like a tank, but moved like a rally car.

In the plush backseat, Annabeth's tablet HD screen streamed the latest video and news. Lots of video, but little additional news.

Daegen, seated on the seat beside her, enjoyed the cool breeze from the console-mounted air-con.

Maggie contacted the Atlanta PD and used her connections with the Council of Four and Jace Burrell's name to get through to the Commissioner. He made the introductions to the police Captain on site and in charge of the perimeter.

Alerted, Captain Johnny Joe Carmine waited at the barrier on South Peachtree. When the SUV pulled forward, he ordered the wooden barricade pulled aside, waving the driver through while ignoring shouted questions from the press.

When told who she would meet, Annabeth imagined, based only on his name, a white man with a cultural background crossed between southern roots and Italian heritage. The back door opened and a tall African-American in the Captain's uniform of the Atlanta Police Department looked in and stopped dead still. He was face-to-face with a black German Shepherd with large white teeth.

"Daegen, get in the back so the Captain and I can talk," Annabeth said.

The dog gave the man a meaningful look, making sure he understood how near he would remain, and then jumped between the seat-backs.

"Please have a seat, Captain Carmine," the vampire said. "No one will bite you."

Cap in hand, the policeman settled in the seat beside the red-head, the dog's muzzle in his peripheral vision.

"Ms. Hughes, I do not think you should consider interfering," he said. "When those people took over the mall and placed hostages in danger, they became a police matter."

"I understand, Captain. But I am the Vampire Directorate's Overlord for this territory." She purposely used the Vampire Directorate instead of Burrell's name. It added weight. A lot of weight. "Those people now answer to me, though they do not seem fully aware of that reality. This lurid attempt to force the release of Arina Kishka is shameful. I will not allow it to proceed. We certainly will not release Arina."

"The FBI have taken control," he informed her.

"Then please introduce me to the FBI agent in charge."

It required three SUVs to transport the team and equipment from Annabeth's new compound to the parking lot behind a row of shops three blocks from the mall. The shops were closed, boarded up, and for sale.

Unlike Annabeth, when they departed the drivers turned and headed for the private airport. Expecting watchers to report to those at the mall, they hoped the move would indicate people being transported to leave, or cars being sent to collect people arriving. Either way, it would not warn them of a team on their way downtown.

Once the drivers were sure no one followed, they rerouted for the staging area.

"Everyone grab your equipment and weapons," Quan ordered. "We're going through the tunnel Tom located on the city diagram from here to a block from the Deluxe. It places us inside the police barricades. At that point Simone will lead. Stay in a close bunch. She will spell the area and we should go undetected into the rear entrance of the hotel."

Kristy returned to report finding the store with access to the tunnel. She forced the back door and left it open. Maggie had remotely disabled alarms. The drivers remained to guard the vehicles. The group in gray, and one in business-suit blue, began their mission.

They walked silently along a dank maintenance tunnel, and found the embedded ladder to the access grate located on a sidewalk above. Simone took the lead, using her air-magic to lift the heavy grate and set it aside. She cast her spell as she completed the climb.

Nine wraiths followed her out of the hole and then grouped behind her as she covered the short distance to the rear entrance of the Deluxe.

The police had forced employees and guests to evacuate the building. A team of FBI agents monitored the Mall from a room on the third story, but no one bothered to post sentries below. No one bothered to lock the doors after leaving under duress either.

With the downtown area sealed off and the buildings cleared, Quan's team reached the downstairs bar without a glitch.

Ambient light from neon signage and backlighting from bottle displays provided sufficient illumination. They had night-vision goggles with them, but the high-tech systems were not yet required.

Simone cast airwaves through the room, but none of the zephyrs escaped. She followed Quan through double doors to offices and storage rooms, casting more air currents into each space. In the room holding wine racks, several breaths escaped through the wall behind a wooden rack holding expensive red wines.

McWaters and Campbell handed bottles to Michele and Kristy until the shelves were empty. The two men lifted the structure and carried it aside. Simone ran her hand across the exposed wooden slat wall now exposed. Within seconds she stepped away, murmured a spell, and the wall opened toward them on rusted hinges.

"Maggie, this is Michele. We have a corridor between the hotel and the mall. If it's passable, we should be in the mall's basement in a few minutes."

Maggie passed the news to Annabeth, who stood before a man in an inexpensive grey suit, white shirt, and blue-and-red striped necktie.

"Special Agent Oswald, I am not attempting to question your authority," she said. Her green eyes held the FBI agent's attention. She was neither afraid nor impressed by his credentials. "I realize this is a hostage situation. I know your primary goal is to have those hostages released unharmed. I am offering you a chance for exactly that."

"I cannot let a civilian walk in there," he said. "You are not trained for this."

"I am not a civilian, Special Agent Oswald. I am the Overlord. The humans, thralls, and vampires who have taken those hostage are now my responsibility. If they harm innocents, the damage done to human-vampire relations will take years to repair. With respect, Special Agent Oswald, you have no idea what I am trained to do. Do not let my appearance confuse you. Vampires exist for thousands of years. We have many skills developed over many centuries."

Annabeth Hughes never received anything akin to hostage negotiating instruction, and was not one of the older vampires. She did not actually claim either point, but allowed the FBI Special Agent to believe what he wished.

"You think they will listen to you?"

"I think it will cost us nothing to try," she replied. "I will walk up to the front door and ask to speak with the vampires in command. I will give them the opportunity to walk away from this stupidity. If they accept me as their Overlord, everything will return to normal. If they refuse, I will walk away."

"They are demanding Arina Kishka," he said. "Will the Council return her?"

"If you allow me to speak with them, and I cannot reason with the leaders, I will certainly contact the Council and report the situation from my perspective."

"If she isn't turned over, we may have to go in with force," he warned.

"So be it," she replied.

"The FBI, nor local law enforcement can be responsible for your protection if you go in there," he said, capitulating to the logic of her argument.

"Understood. I will be back shortly," she said, turning and heading for the mall entrance, the black dog at her side.

"Maggie, I'm on the way to the entrance."

Simone used magic to blast an opening though the concrete wall and into the basement below the mall. She deadened the sound, and held the debris in the air, setting it down softly in a corner of the dark space.

"Better than C4," Toole said.

"Night vision," Quan ordered. "Maggie says Annabeth is on her way to the mall entrance. I don't see any stairs or ladders. We have to make our own way to the first level. Kristy, you look the lightest. Get on Toole's shoulders and check the ceiling."

"Concrete," the pilot called down. "I don't sense anything like an access. They simply abandoned this section of the basement."

Quan handed her four lines of shaped explosive putty and a remote detonator. "Make a square big enough for us to crawl through," she ordered. "Toole, get her over against the West wall. There should be open floor space above us at that location."

Kristy kept one hand against the ceiling for balance as the security agent walked slowly to the side wall, making sure not to stumble by stepping on loose debris.

The young woman jumped down and said, "Lines are set and detonator in and on," she reported.

The group hurried to the eastern wall. Simone placed a barrier of air between them and the rest of the basement. She cast a sound block to envelope the area below and above the explosion, and nodded to Quan.

"Fire in the hole," she announced and pressed the remote detonator.

A flash; followed by the dust and cobwebs shaking free from the ceiling. A square section of concrete lay shattered on the floor.

"Wow," Tom said. "You really did cover the sound."

"If you liked that, you'll love what comes next," Simone replied.

What came next? The Air Witch used her control of the element to levitate each team member up and through the opening. Michele going first to secure the engineering studio before allowing others to follow.

"Maggie, we've breeched the mall."

"Annabeth, the team is inside."

"Got it," the vampire whispered as she strode up the flight of steps toward the right side double-doors of the main entry and exit from the center.

Daegen walked on her right side. While not on a leash, he did sport a black harness. Under his chest a special holster held a Beretta PX4 Subcompact 9mm. With a barrel length of only three-inches, the thirteen-round (plus one in the chamber) pistol packed a punch. German Shepherds rarely have to go through pat-downs. Should anything bad start, she had easy access to a weapon. Two, when you count the canine.

Before she could knock or yell for attention, a hastily written number on a sheet of paper was pressed against the glass. The hand holding it disappeared between upturned benches repurposed to barricade the entrance.

She read the ten-digits.

"Whoever is in charge is smarter than I considered," she told Dae. She pulled an expensive smart phone from the pocket of her slacks and dialed the number.

"Unless you're here to provide a timetable for Arina's return, go away," a male voice answered.

"I'm here to give you the chance to obey my orders before I have to do something more violent," she replied.

"We know who you are, Annabeth Hughes," the male said. "We do not recognize you as sovereign."

"Then you do not recognize Jace Burrell or the Vampire Directorate as sovereign either."

"We do not. Arina Kishka is my sire, For more than ten-thousand-years I have followed her. The others with me have done so for one-to-seven-thousand years. You cannot supplant such loyalty in one night," he said.

"Then you are Diego Haas," she said. "Arina's first turned. You are experienced enough to know you are taking a dangerous position, Diego."

"And you are Bishop's Bitch," Haas returned. "The Vampire Directorate and the Council of Four refuse to recognize the danger all non-humans face. Technology has been allowed to advance without restraints. Humans have shown a lack of moral concern among their own cultures. How do you expect them to act toward vampires when they realize how much power they wield? Arina sees the future clearly. If another human-vampire war is coming, it is best for our side to act first."

"Fanaticism will not prevent the rise of humans," Annabeth said. She spoke calmly, a counter-balance to Haas' strident tone. "You are a small group. You do not represent all of Arina's coterie. The other vampires will not act preemptively.

"Let the hostages go, Diego. You have placed yourself and the others in a no-win situation. Accept me as your Overlord and we can begin rebuilding the relationships between us and the humans who share this territory."

A harsh laugh answered her heartfelt request.

"You are a child lecturing a god," he said. "Vampires will do what they must to survive. If taking control of this planet is the only answer to our continued existence, then so be it. Go back to London."

Haas disconnected. Annabeth pivoted and headed back toward the police barricades.

"Maggie, tell Michele and Simone to go. The vampires in the mall have no intention of letting the hostages go. They plan on slaughtering them."

"Will do, but I heard the call," Maggie replied. "Why do you think they are going to kill those people?"

"He hung up without repeating the demand for Arina's release," the young Overlord answered. "They never expected it. This will be a bloody show for television and the internet. Vampires mercilessly butchering and feeding on defenseless men, women, and children."

"They want to start a cross-species war?"

"Yes, and I may have moved the timetable up by confronting them."

Chapter 13

While waiting to make their next move, Michele Quan silently reevaluated her team members.

Simone Sinclair, a powerful air elemental Legacy Witch. Her magic provided a force multiplier, improving the odds of the team against an enemy with greater numbers and their own supernatural talents. She was also a person more comfortable leading than following. Would she follow Michele's orders, or go rogue at a crucial moment?

She knew Tom Farway. The former Royal Marine would be reliable, but he was older and away from action for more than a decade.

Kristy Nichol best described as unknown. As a Council pilot she would have received defensive combat training, but she came across as possessing more skills than she admitted to.

James McWaters and Harry Campbell were solid blokes. Younger than Farway, both had similar military backgrounds. While less removed from active duty than Tom, they also spent their previous years flying luxury jets, not in the trenches.

Rusty Toole, former US Marine with an attitude, seemed to handle himself well. If his cockiness came from confidence and not conceit, he would support his team.

Camila Raoul graduated the US Army Rangers' school before opting for a private security job. Her credentials were top flight. She baled on the Army because she felt slighted as a female. Quan understood Raoul's disappointment.

The other two security agents she hired away, Sommers and Franco, stayed behind to protect their rear. Franco positioned in the basement while Sommers remained at the hotel bar. The quick records check by Maggie gave them high marks for professionalism, but neither had real battle experience. Until she knew them better, having them take back-up positions made the most sense.

"Michele, Annabeth is walking away," Maggie's voice interrupted Quan's internal review. "She thinks the vamps inside don't care about Arina. This is about starting a war by slaughtering innocents and broadcasting it live. She also thinks they might move their plan up."

"Roger," Michele replied. "Maggie, open communications between all team members. From this point forward, everybody hears everything. Do you have eyes on the corridors?"

"First level has fifteen Bad Guys scattered around the hallway, and another six at the front entrance. I count four at the entrance to the restaurant, and movement in the restaurant, but no eyes-on," the tech reported.

"Second level is locked-down storefronts on either side of a center aisle. Open at either end where the escalators are located. Twelve Bad Guys acting bored. Some are actually window shopping," she told everyone.

"The third level has law office at the South end over the restaurant. One BG (Bad Guy) at the entrance. I've seen two vampires go in and out a couple of times."

"Confirmed as vampires?" Michele interrupted.

"It's how they move," Maggie replied. "Architect is next with two humans. App developer has two humans, and so does the fitness studio. I rewound tapes from the earlier delivery. The second delivery of crates, all eight, were taken into the fitness center."

"They must have guards on the loading bays and the garage entrance," Michele said.

"I don't see any," the tech replied. "There are satchels attached to the doors. If anyone tries to breech the mall from there, things will go boom."

"Simone, Kristy, Toole, and Raoul. You are Team One. Raoul, you are team leader," Quan told them. She did not explain her choices. The others recognized she combined those with similar training, and selected Raoul because of her Ranger experience. "You will neutralize every body between here and the restaurant as quickly as possible. Simone, the others will plow your path to the hostages. I want you in the restaurant as quickly as possible. I don't care if you use witchcraft, fieldcraft, or Kraft mac and cheese. Get inside and do what you can to protect those people. When it's safe, deliver them to the Bobbies."

"I thought we didn't want the vamps up top to see hostages set loose on tv," Toole said.

Michele ignored him.

"Tom, James, and Harry are with me. We exit and go left. Plan on hitting the second floor weapons hot. The targets will be set up inside the hallway like on a range. No hesitation. I want every bad guy in the corridor taken down," she ordered.

Three heads nodded in understanding and approval.

"Tom and I will take the far escalator to the third level and cover the law firm. Camila, Rusty, and Simone will join us there as soon as the restaurant is cleared. Kristy, you will watch their backs. Keep the escalator steps empty."

She turned to her other Team Two members. "Harry and James will go up the nearest escalator. Do what you can to secure the gym. Get eyes on those eight crates as soon as you can."

"The app developer and the architect?" McWater asked.

"One of you keep an eye on the corridor. As soon as we can free people, I will send them to you, clearing the other businesses on the way."

"The hostages on tv?" Toole asked, repeating his concern.

"Maggie, we go in five-minutes from my mark," she said aloud. She watched the sweep-second hand on her watch, waited , and said, "Mark. At four-minutes-fifty-seconds kill the electricity in the building."

"It will wipe out cctv, too," Maggie replied.

"I know, but, other than the vampires, and possibly the older thralls, darkness is our best weapon," Michele answered. "We have night-vision goggles."

"That's why you added flash-suppressors to the long guns," Tom said. "They won't be able to aim at muzzle blasts. Well planned."

"It's still eight against eighty," Quan reminded them. "Go heavy on the fire. No point in carrying loaded clips home."

At four-minutes Quan ordered, "Team One on the door. When the lights go, you go. Simone, I don't know what a Legacy Witch is capable of magically, but whatever you can do, please don't hold back."

"Didn't plan to," the French-Canadian sorceress answered.

"Team Two, be ready to follow Team One. Everyone place googles on. Close your eyes and turn them on. When I say the word, the lights will be off."

The room became eerily still. Then the lights disappeared.

Chapter 14

Oberon stood beside Titania. She overshadowed her powerful husband. Her blood-red leathers covering her curves from neck to toes. The red low-heel boots matching perfectly. Gladius, a double-edge sword favored by gladiators, strapped to her waist. A dirk sheathed on her opposite hip. A cold steel Italian dagger, twelve-inches and sharp strapped to her right calf.

As a Titan, the steel of the blades did not affect her the way they would someone fully Fae. They would be deadly against Fairy, Seelie or UnSeelie, who could not stand the touch of iron or the razor edges.

Her auburn hair contained into two lengthy braids. The dark red tresses nearly the shade of her clothing. She held her leather-wrapped helmet in her hand.

"You look like Little John and Little Orphan Annie had a weird love-child," Cahal said to Skerrit.

In his humanoid form, the Fae hunter stood six-six and weighed twenty-one stones. His fire-red hair pulled tight to his skull and tied into a pony-tail with a leather strap. Several leather laces then encircled the tail to keep it from interfering when he fought.

The smile he gave the shorter part-Fae gleamed white between a red mustache and beard. The beard also held by two straps.

"Could notta picked better parents meself," he answered the jibe.

His fawn-colored leather vest left massive, muscled arms exposed, the forearms covered by leather greaves with silver filigree. He wore gloves without fingers. Leather britches covered his large legs. Steel-toed boots on his feet.

"Steel-toes?" Cahal asked.

"Iron doesn't bother a centaur," Skerrit replied. "When I change, my hooves are clad in steel with steel horseshoes. Nothing better for tearing apart a Fae opponent."

The quiver across his back carried arrows with steel or silver tips. Skerrit's quiver never ran dry. Every arrow fired was magically replaced. His bow, a recurve design based on the Hun's weapon, was lashed to the quiver.

Cahal looked closer and said, "Your bow is Velcroed to the quiver."

"Faster than tying a strap, and quicker than a buckle," the centaur responded. "Nothing wrong with mixing magic and technology."

For his part, Cahal wore black tactical combat clothing. Over his long-sleeved shirt was a Kevlar vest with a tactical knife in cross-pull. Vest pockets held a variety of items, from compact explosive cylindrical discs to metal flechettes of steel. The shuriken could be thrown singularly or in a group.

His pants were reinforced in the crotch and inner thighs with Kevlar, to protect vital areas from excessive damage. He would look as if he wore riding jodhpurs except for the two 9mm pistols strapped into thigh holsters. The Sherpa designed holsters perfect for fast draws. Eight additional clips rode quick-release holders on his belt. A Cerrullan sword and sheath was carried across his back. The blue-metal from the planet Cerrul, the non-terrestrial vampires' home world. Nothing ever stood against the sword's edge and survived.

Morgan joined them in her own black leathers. She carried a variety of knives and swords.

Before Cahal could comment, Oberon ordered them to follow. He pressed a hidden release, and a doorway appeared behind the King's throne.

"You're about to learn a secret you must never reveal, Cahal," Morgan whispered as they went last through the portal and began down narrow steps.

Moonstones lit the stairwell. Torches illuminated a cavernous chamber at the bottom of the steps. Fin Bheara waited with three-dozen Fae warriors. He saluted his liege by placing his right fist against his left chest and bowing.

Behind Fin and the warriors a chasm gaped in a stone wall.

"The eighth gate," Morgan whispered. "The only one on the planet operating in both directions. It joins Earth and Tir na Nog, the Fae home world. Only Fae use this passage."

Fin Bheara wore perfectly matching white leather top and pants. They appeared as a one-piece uniform. Even his knee-high boots matched. He wore a Galea-style helmet with a garnet plume affixed at the crest. A white cape of silk or satin fell from his shoulders to mid-calf, and a garnet belt crossed from waist to right hip where a sword with rapier-cage handle rested.

Behind him the thirty-six Fae were dressed similarly, but without plumes on their helmets. Their uniforms cleaned, oiled, and polished. They gleamed like patent leather one could see a reflection in.

After acknowledging Oberon, he stepped in front of Cahal, removed his helmet, and extend his right hand and arm.

"Whatever my feelings about you or your relatives, I want you to know those emotions do not go with me onto the battlefield. When you need me and my warriors, we will be there."

Cahal grasped the proffered forearm. Eye to eye with the Royal, he said, "You realize your warriors look like Imperial Storm Troopers."

Bheara smiled, pulled Cahal closer, and whispered, "Where do you think Lucas got the idea?"

"If you begin from an exit portal on Earth, the journey will require several gates changes," Oberon told them. "Besides the two-way direct passage, one entry and one exit gate exist on Tir na Nog. By using our exit gate you will halve the number of connections required to reach Pandaemonium."

"And make it easier for the Black Queen to find the way back," Skerrit said. "Do you think this a good idea, Oberon?"

"Getting there and taking Sionnach away from her is the most important thing," he answered. "Sooner is better. The entry gate on Tir na Nog is heavily warded by magic and guarded by powerful Fae. Plus I hope our three warriors are able to find a way to destroy her."

"Fin Bheara, his troop, and I will be with you until the final gate," Morgan said. "If anyone follows you, they will find a surprise waiting. If you need us on Pandaemonium, and you are able to send a message, we will come."

"Does the Black Queen not have her gates warded?" Skerrit asked.

"She does," Oberon said. He walked to Cahal side, took the young man's left arm, and lifted his hand. "Do you know how to use this ring?" he asked.

"Yes," Cahal replied. The silver ring on his ring-finger did, as he understood it, two things. Placed against a barrier, when he spoke an incantation taught him by Simone, a warded gate would open. At least gates warded by Legacy Witches. It also, supposedly, contained the magic within him. Magic which traditionally traveled from female to female only.

"I don't know if it will work on a ward not placed by a Legacy," he added.

"It will," the King replied. "Sionnach has a similar ring and it allowed us to enter the Black Queen's world."

"We only concern ourselves with the need to avoid a million UnSeelie, slip by the Black Queen unnoticed, find Sionnach, escape the prison he is held in, make our way back through UnSeelie hoards, likely alerted of the escape, and plane-travel back home," Titania said. Her words delivered without sarcasm. The steps required for success clearly defined and entirely improbable.

"A million?" Skerrit asked.

"A low estimate," Oberon said.

"I hope so," the centaur rejoined. "Otherwise Titania and Cahal will have nothing to do."

Chapter 15

Plane-travel is rarely easy.

Cahal stepped through one portal to find a lush timberland beneath a grey, cloudless sky. Titania, who exited before him, sparred with a ten-foot-tall cross between a grizzly bear and a lion. The beast raised up on hind legs, had a long tail and front paws with claws like a big cat. The tremendous snouted-head held grizzly-sized teeth. Titania kept it at bay with her gladius, thrusting to nick the animal, then quickly stepping away.

"I think she's making it mad," Skerrit said, stepping beside Cahal. "How far to the exit gate?"

"Three-miles west," the Dúnmharú said.

Bheara stepped onto the world, appraised the situation, and pulled his sword. As he rushed to join the fight, the centaur's big right hand grabbed his billowing cape and yanked him back.

"The Queen would not appreciate an intervention without a request," he told his fellow Royal.

The animal bent down and forward, baring teeth and spat a half-growl and half-roar into Titania's face.

The last of the Titans slapped the beast with a backhand across its snout and returned her own roar. It was, frankly, titanic.

Startled, perhaps tired of the many pinpricks, and obviously outnumbered, the creature turned and trotted into the dense forest.

"Bearion," Skerrit whispered to Cahal. "Whaddah you think, lad? Good name?"

Four gates later they wasted two-hours negotiating with a race of short bipedal aliens. Their world several dimensions and a galaxy away from Earth. The spokesperson for a group of the orange-colored, fur covered species used hand gestures and facial expressions to indicate payment was required to enter their world. Also, payment for transportation to the exit, which it indicated sat far away; and (Ready for it?) payment to exit.

The final cost amounted to three leather belts, two white capes, and one silver-decorated dagger and sheath. The exit portal, which turned out to be less than one-mile distant, took them to a dark, desolate place with barely enough oxygen in its atmosphere for them to survive a trek across a valley and half-way up the side of an embankment.

Working their way up the steep slope toward a cave entrance and the exit, Skerrit, laboring beside Cahal, said, "This was Oberon's shorter route. Can you imagine what the long way would have been like?"

The final stop before Pandaemonium placed them on a plateau of dirt and shrub grass. Mountains framed the horizon behind them, and a glassy lake lay at the base on one side of the mesa. They crossed to enter a flatland of high grass, making their way through the weeds, using swords as machetes, until they reached another, steeper plateau. Rough-hewn steps rose from the flatland to the tableland above.

"I've seen no signs of civilization," Cahal said.

"I've seen no animal life," Bheara said.

"These steps were carved a long time ago," Morgan said, running a hand across a chiseled riser. "The race who shaped these steps could be extinct."

"Or watching and waiting to attack," Bheara said, his eyes casting over the sea of weeds. "We are within one gate of the Black Witch."

"And where we part ways," Titania said. "Fin, you have the watch I gave you?"

The Royal warrior extracted a gold pocket watch from a utility pouch on his belt. He opened the cover, examined the piece, and told his Queen, "It is working perfectly."

"We do not know how the days and nights work on this planet. You must time our absence by your watch," she said. "If we are not in contact in forty-eight-hours, return to Tir na Nog and tell Oberon to either prepare an attack or a defense. You are not to follow us into Pandaemonium. We cannot afford to lose our finest warriors on another wasted rescue attempt."

"Do you honestly expect us to leave our Queen?" the Maerrighan asked.

"I'm ordering you to, Morrigan," the response. "But I have no intention of failing. Be prepared to fight when we return. The exit from Pandaemonium will not bring us directly back. We will make one other gate transfer. If we are followed you will be fighting in the grasslands. You will defend and retreat to the exit gate near those mountains."

All eyes turned to the peaks. They did not appear particularly near.

"Plan your defense and retreat, Fin," Titania said. "Make the environment your asset. If there are obstacles between the entry and exit gates, find them and make plans to get around them. Take whatever time you have to prepare."

"Of course, your Highness," Bheara replied with a slight bow. "May I make a suggestion?"

"Please," Titania replied.

"The Dúnmharú's mixed heritage may shield him from immediate detection by the UnSeelie, but his dress and armaments will make them curious. I suggest he take my cloak. He can use it to conceal his appearance."

"Smart," Cahal said. He took the white cape and tied the collar around his neck. He pulled the cloth around him, holding it at his chest with one hand.

"That will work," the Queen said. "We will share a meal before we exit."

"Felinursa," Skerrit said to Cahal. "Get it? Feline and Ursa for bear."

Cahal ignored him, walking away to find a comfortable place to rest.

When faced with having to plane-travel to cross the globe in time to save Roxanne, the Australian-based Legacy Witch, from death by Blood Dragon, Cahal's grandmother revealed a secret.

He wore a silver ring etched with runes. The vampire Bishop gave it to him, instructing him to never take it off. Simone informed him it acted to contain wild magic within his soul. It also allowed him to channel spells. He used it on Earth to open two warded gates and stop the Blood Dragons from murdering Roxanne.

With Titania and Skerrit standing behind him, he placed his left palm against an invisible wall of Fae magic blocking their exit. He whispered, "Müēc yād öd met wō müēc yād yart." As on Earth, the magic yielded.

"That could have set off an alarm," the centaur said, stepping though an open doorway and onto a field of yellow flowers.

"Place your hand back where the wall was," Titania ordered him. "Say the spell, but say it backward. Each word backward."

Placing his palm in the approximate location of the original ward was easy. Turning the gibberish around and repeating everything backward demanded intense concentration.

Slowly, carefully, he said, "Tray day ceum ow tem do day ceum."

The ward reappeared. Cahal stood with his eyes focused far beyond the doorway.

"What is it, lad?" Skerrit asked.

"I spoke phonetically," he answered. "But what I said was tredecim autem duedecim."

"Sounds the same to me," the Fae said, waiting for a more reasonable reason for standing there.

"It's a variation of ancient Latin. I said thirteen of twelve."

"Whatever you said worked," the big man said. "Can we get going before something comes to see why the ward dropped?"

"Sure. Any suggestions which way?"

"The big black castle to our left might be a good start," Titania told them.

The two males turned to the direction she peered. A copy of Oberon's castle sat atop a rise perhaps five-miles distant. No village surrounding it, and the exterior completely black, it represented a near-perfect negative of the one on Earth.

"It doesn't have any windows," Cahal said.

"Then maybe she won't see us coming," Titania said, taking the first step toward the home of the Black Queen.

Chapter 16

Simone could have used magic to improve her vision in the dark, but why waste the energy? No one would notice the fashion gaff; night vision goggles - big, bulky, and effective - with a designer outfit. She walked quickly toward the far end of the corridor and the restaurant, her hands up and her element ready for her call.

Camila Raoul followed the witch, one step back and on the woman's right side. This allowed her an open lane of fire as she carried the FN FS2000 CQB 5.56 in her right hand. The short automatic combat rifle light and deadly. Trusting her ability, she set it for single fire.

Toole, similarly armed, moved across the hallway, then forward with his left side against the wall.

Kristy held back and covered their six. If they met resistance, they would change their attack based on the situation.

Two bodies stood twenty-feet from the entrance, on Toole's side. A single body stood ten-feet in front of Simone and Camila, his back to their approach.

Raoul fired first. Head shot dropped her target. The suppressor silenced the report and prevented a muzzle flare. Toole took his targets one-second later. His FN set for three-shot bursts. One of the targets dropped a long weapon, which made a loud crack when it landed.

"What was that?" asked a voice near the front entrance reacting to the bodies hitting the floor. A half-dozen BGs congregated at the security kiosk and information desk in the center of the corridor. Simone prepared to place a protective barrier of condensed air between them and the potential of incoming rounds. Before she could call the spell the three operators opened fire. The wisp-sounds of bullets exiting the short barrels mixed with the impact thuds as they found their marks. Groans and short gasps of pain followed.

As the four neared, two of the downed targets slowly began to rise. Radios called out as concerned guards further down the corridor asked for a report.

Raoul lifted her rifle, prepared to take the two survivors out, when a green-tinted Kristy flashed into her sight. The pilot closed, her FN tossed on its leash and across her back. A wicked matte-finished blade in her hand caught the first guy across his neck as he pushed himself into a squat.

As the target's hands went to his neck, he was already falling backward. Kristy completed the slash and brought the knife around and drove it into the skull of the female who had made it to her knees.

"Thralls," Kristy said over the closed com. "Nine down. I count six running this way."

Simone ran forward, surprising her escort, already startled by the decisive action of the Council pilot.

"Get down, Kristy," Simone said. "I'm going to blow out their eardrums."

The pilot dropped as the witch pressed her palms forward and then pretended to squeeze them together. Six people screamed, bodies twisting in different directions as they reacted to the air pressure inside their heads exploding.

From her prone position, Kristy, FN back in hand, fired and ended their misery . . . permanently. Raoul reached the security kiosk and added her fire power. Toole swept the front entrance to make sure no other Bad Guys hid in the recesses.

While Kristy regained her feet, Raoul kicked open the door to the security office situated behind the kiosk. A green-lit body raised up from a seat in front of a dead wall of television screens. Double tap and two 5.56mm NATO rounds dropped her on the floor. With the awareness of thralls now in her head, she waited to make sure the woman did not recover from the kill shots.

Sure the body would remain a body, she backed out of the office. Toole stood between the kiosk and the front doors, eyes south. The former Army Ranger followed his stare to see Simone and Kristy headed for the restaurant at a full sprint. She realized what they already had. The guards would recognize a full attack was on. The hostages were in immediate peril. She went from standstill to full sprint in seconds. Toole caught and kept pace on her left.

Racing after the two women, she notice Simone's expensive shoes lying on the floor. The witch would not allow anything to slow her down. The Ranger's heart thumped harder, but not from the exertion of the sprint. She experienced a wave of pride in being on a team with someone so determined to save lives. As for Ms. Kristy Nichol. When this was over, if she lived, she intended to find out a lot more about the quiet pilot who could shoot better than her, and handled a combat knife like a pro.

"Left, last storefront," Raoul called, seeing someone stepping from the store.

"Black outfit," Toole responded. He stopped, braced, and fired. The body dropped. Now he had work to do to catch the three women.

Simone, aided by a tail wind and sailing across the floor, arrived at the restaurant entrance first. She barreled past the greeter's dais. Unlike the rest of the first floor, the windows allowed a lot of light to stream into the open area. It overwhelmed the night-vision goggles, forcing the witch to close her eyes before she yanked at the strap holding the apparatus to her face.

A man in black stepped from around the corner and aimed a pistol at the blonde's head, finger already beginning to squeeze the trigger.

Kristy, having tossed her goggles before entering the restaurant, caught the guy with a body block, throwing her weight into his midsection. The bullet tore into the wall across from Simone.

"Close your eyes," Simone ordered as Raoul came to a stop beside her, and Toole followed. Both had their goggles hanging around their necks.

An incantation caused the moisture in the air to expand into crystals. The crystals amplified the ambient light entering through the glass windows, and then burst into a brilliant flash.

Unprepared, the hostages and those holding them were temporarily blinded.

Eyes open, Toole and Raoul marked the four people in black standing at four corners of the restaurant. Each held a machine gun or shot gun in one hand while the other hand rubbed furious-ly at scalded eyes.

The two security agents wasted no time taking them out.

Toole advanced to make sure the downed were corpses and not thralls or vampires while Raoul covered the area in case someone hidden jumped out. Kristy lifted herself away from the man she tackled. Blood gushed from a gaping wound in his neck.

"Another thrall?" Raoul asked.

"Don't know," the pilot answered. "It was the fastest way to end the argument."

While they secured the area, Simone used magic to calm the hostages. She relieved the pain from the burst of light, warmed their skin, and sent soothing scents over zephyrs. She also used the air to carry her words to each of them, assuring them they were now safe.

"This is Team One," Raoul said over the com. "First level is secure. Hostages safe. Team is whole."

Quan exited through the stairwell door to the second level, ri-fle up. She immediately juked left. Farway followed and covered the right quadrant. McWaters came through allowing Farway to advance. Campbell came last, closed the door and placed his back against it.

The escalators limited line-of-sight down the center of the cor-ridor, but Quan and Farway could see all the way to the escalators at the North end of the mall. Shuttered shops along both sides were dark.

Campbell remained back, taking a position beside the escala-tor housing where he could watch the stairwell door. His angle also allowed him to provide cover for the other team members as they advanced.

They began a leap-frog push forward. Three rifles trained on the hallway ahead as each one took turns moving forward. With-out any cover, the rear member stood, the center rested on one knee, and the foremost shooter prone. As the last in line moved ahead, the shooter on a knee stood, and the one lying on the floor, came up to a knee. Once the mover stopped and assumed a prone position, they waited for any response. A few seconds of quiet, and the dance repeated.

Michele Quan dropped to her stomach fifteen-feet from the twin escalator housings when eight figures stepped around each side of the transporters. She triggered her automatic FN, but too late for McWaters. Standing thirty-feet behind her, he received several hits.

"Aim for their heads," she ordered. The ambushers were not wearing night-vision equipment, but had zeroed in on McWaters in the center of the darkened corridor. They were vampires or thralls. Either way, difficult to kill. If any were full vampires, only taking off a head or completely bleeding them out would keep them down.

She clicked her FN to three-tap bursts and framed her sights on above the shoulders. A hit to the heart would also kill a thrall, but they could be using body armor.

Bullets tore into the ceramic floor. Chips of tile slashed her face as enemy fire closed on her position. Behind her she heard Farway's response. Further back, she heard Campbell's FN on full automatic as he tried to cover them by spraying fire above their lower silhouettes at the BGs standing on either side of the corridor.

Quan did not bother rolling since there was nothing to roll behind. She concentrated on marking and taking out targets. In her ear she heard, "This is Team One. First level is secure. Hostages safe. Team is whole."

A lull in the firing gave her a moment to switch her magazine. A glimpse backward and she saw Tom's crumpled body first, then McWater's. Campbell remained by the escalators, using the minimal cover they provided. He was not firing either.

She decided to roll to her right and place her body against the wall beneath a display window. Bullets had already shattered the display glass, but most of it fell into the store. Shards crunched beneath her, but did not penetrate the heavy cloth of her combat wear. The position limited her vision to one side of the North escalators, but shielded her on one side.

They had put down the eight attackers, but she could see two begin to rise. Hit, but not head shots.

"This is Quan," she radioed. "Heavy fire. Two members down. Vampires or thralls at the North escalators on the second level. Eyes on two mobile on the eastern quad. Harry, stay back. Do not come forward for me. Do not let them use the stairwell or escalators to box us in."

"Copy," Campbell replied. "None of the bodies on the western side have moved, but I see four more moving up. They will clear the housing in less than five-seconds."

Michele decided to use her time to line up on the two undead returning to the fight. If Harry could hold the newcomers long enough, she might be able to scramble forward and place the escaltor's housing between her and them.

Before she pulled the trigger, four bodies flew forward and high. "Can vampires fly?" she asked herself.

"Team One is now on level two, please don't shoot us," Camila Raoul called.

Committed to the act, Quan placed three 5.56mm jacketed slugs into the head of one mark as the four air-born baddies began screaming and tearing at their own heads.

Kristy Nichol stepped behind the second mark and used two hands to drive a knife through the crown of its skull.

Simone appeared with her hands clasped together and her eyes blazing in the eerie image created by the ambient light the goggles amplified. Raoul rushed around the witch and finished the four remaining targets executioner style.

"Look out!" Kristy yelled at Harry Campbell. He had stepped forward as Raoul completed neutralizing the threats.

Quick reflexes for a man out of active service for a number of years saved him. He turned and raised the short-barrel FN CQB in time for it to catch the sword's blade.

The tempered steel slashed through the composite material of the weapon, leaving a gash in the metal barrel.

There was no mistaking what attacked. Fangs fully extended, the tall, thin silhouette blended with the darkness around him. The assault thwarted, the force of the blow still sent Campbell reeling backward. The pilot's subcompact rifle useless, and without time to pull a back-up as the vampire moved to finish the strike.

At the other end of the corridor rifles raised, but Campbell stood between them and the vampire. Simone needed time to cast a spell, and there was no time.

Campbell could see the beautifully crafted rapier rise. He noted the complex metal cage work on the hilt. Details becoming vivid as his life was about to end.

His senses expanded by the enormity of the moment, he saw the tip of a blade appear above the vampire's right shoulder. It disappeared and reappeared over his left shoulder, and then was gone again.

The vampire froze, his black-filled eyes widened. His eyelids drooped, and his head slid forward, falling from his shoulders to bounce on the ceramic floor. The tall, lean body fell into itself. Melting, instead of collapsing, to cover the severed head.

Annabeth Hughes stood there. Feet apart with the long, slender blade held tip-down. Behind her Daegen kept watch on the non-functioning escalator connecting the levels. No one else would be sneaking down.

Chapter 17

The black dog sat in the middle of the road. From a distance, it appeared to have no head. As the three neared they could see the hound held its head low, hanging over a wide chest. The shoulder blades extended upward and the uniform black color of the canine is why it appeared headless from a distance.

It watched them approach, distrustful black eyes beneath lowered lids. The long head and droopy ears of a hound, but one weighing over three-hundred pounds. If it stood, the front shoulders would rise four-feet above the ground. Seated, a whiplash black tail curled around its front paws, more feline than canine.

"Yeth Hound," Skerrit said. "Haven't seen one in thousands of years. Fantastic hunters, and smart. Hounds what use scent and sight. Fae used them to hunt dragons. Epona, a Fae Royal who protected horses and dogs, took the last of the Yeth and left Tir na Nog."

"No one has seen Epona since," Titania added. "She was a kind, gentle soul. She would have nothing to do with the Black Queen."

"Before she went bad, the Black Queen did have a soft spot for dogs," the centaur said. "She bred some bloody huge ones to guard her home."

"What is this one guarding?" Cahal asked, wrapping Fin's cloak closer to conceal his clothing and weapons.

"Obviously, the road to the Queen's castle," Titania said, stopping short of the seated canine.

The dog stood and displayed its teeth.

"Those are as white as he is black," Skerrit said. "And a lot of them."

From the gullies bordering the road, four more Yeth Hounds emerged. Two on either side.

"Don't react," Cahal said to his companions. "Don't go for any weapons."

He walked toward the first hound. He relaxed his hold on the cape, no longer worried if these animals saw his Earth-clothing. They would not care what he did or did not wear.

At six-two, Cahal stood taller than most. If the hound decided to stand up and place its paws on his shoulders, the long head filled with white teeth would reach well above his head.

He held the back of his right hand forward, palm down, and allowed the dog to sniff. Despite a low growl coming from the beast, Cahal remained calm, slowly pulling his hand away. The dog walked a circle around him, taking long draws through its snout. It completed its survey to stand in front of the Dúnmharú before returning to a sit.

Slowly Cahal reached forward underhanded. He rubbed beneath the dog's jaw, working his hand up and around to briskly scratch its neck behind its skull. The hound's eyes closed and it shivered.

Cahal pulled his hand away and waited. The big black animal sneezed, rose, and trotted off to the side of the road. It disappeared into a gully, followed by the other four.

Titania placed a hand on his shoulder and said, "Nice."

"A dog's a dog," he said. "If I had scratched his butt he would have escorted us to the castle. Because we all have mixed blood, our scent did not alarm them. If there are millions of UnSeelie, I doubt any know everyone here by sight."

"Getting past the Yeth Hounds will go a long way on others ignoring us," Skerrit said.

"Sure," Cahal replied. "Who's going to notice a giant red-headed Robin Hood?"

The next encounter did not go so well.

A mile past the hounds they came to a bridge spanning a moat of boiling, oily liquid. Two trolls stood together in a heated argument, barricading the bridge with their rotund bodies.

"It's my turn," the one on the left with stringy yellow hair and a hairless face, said emphatically.

"There's three of 'em," the other replied, spitting the words, and a good deal of actual spittle, into stringy-hair's face. He had black curly locks locked into place with greasy wax. He also sported a curly black beard. His face dominated by thick lips and a bulbous red nose.

"So?"

"You were next if the next one was two, four, or six," Curly said. "Remember. You said you got next so we would be even-steven. Three ain't an even number."

"That's not what I meant," Stringy yelled. "You be twisting words."

"Do you want the Queen to hear you are a liar?"

"I didn't lie. Give me the female. After I'm done with her, I'll make soup. I'll share it with you."

Curly turned and looked at the three travelers before returning to the argument.

"She's worth those two and a dozen more," he said. "But if you promise me half the soup, I'll go for it."

He extended his hand. Stringy grasped it and gave one big shake.

They faced the three newcomers, and Stringy said, "We can kill you and then eat you, or you can surrender and we will play with you, kill you, and then eat you. Your choice."

"It does not seem a fair payment to cross a bridge," Titania said.

"Payment?" Curly gruffed. "We ain't bridge trolls, Sugarpot. This is the best place to get groceries. You're gonna make a fine soup. The boy will be sandwiches for a week, and the big ugly one will be, well, something. He looks kinda tough and tasteless, but I'm a good cook. I'll find some use."

"I'm as tasty as can be," Skerrit said to the curly haired troll. "You'd be lucky to find out, only today isn't your lucky day."

"Every day is our day," String said. "Besides being great cooks, my brother and I are the strongest beings in the world. We don't want to break your bones before cooking you, but we will," he promised.

"Do you want help?" Cahal asked the tall Fae.

Skerrit answered with a sour frown, walked forward and before either brother could react, he pounded each on the crown of their heads with a single hammer blow from his fists.

Heads shrank between fat shoulders and beady eyes rolled up and disappeared. The two bulky brothers fell unconscious to the ground.

"You did have to knock them out in front of the bridge, didn't you?" Cahal asked as he labored to pull the legs of Stringy, moving the massive body enough for them to get through and onto the span.

"You know, Cahal, I don't remember you being this bitchy when you was a lad," the Hunter said. "I think Bishop might have taught you some bad ways."

"We need to hurry," Titania said, stopping the banter before it could become a distraction. "Someone may notice these two."

"Be hard not to," Skerrit agreed. "But nothing to say another UnSeelie didn't crack them."

"If they were lying about being the strongest dark Fae in this world, maybe," she responded. "If they weren't, then something not of this world took them down."

"Should we throw them in the tar river?" Skerrit asked.

"What do you think of your chances of lifting them and tossing them in?" she asked.

"We best hurry," the centaur said, picking up the pace.

"It's a copy of Oberon's castle, but made of some non-reflective stone," Titania said. The three walked side-by-side as they climbed the steps to the double-doors set into the front wall. "She's attempting to replicate the past while removing any essence of light."

"She was a strong Fae before she went crazy," Skerrit said. "We went on a number of hunts together, and she never shied from the lead. It's a shame someone with such a strong will shattered."

"Sounds as if she was more of an unbending personality than someone with a strong will," Cahal said. "When you believe your position is a right, not a privilege, losing it is losing your anchor in a storm."

"You believe my replacing her as the Queen affected her more than losing Oberon's love?" Titania asked.

"Yep," he replied. The more time he spent in the company of the auburn-haired Fae, the less he thought of her as Queen and the more she became companion. His casual tone when speaking to her reflected his ease. That she seemed to not notice made it obvious she had reached a similar level of comfort with him.

"Makes more sense than losing a lover," Skerrit said. He made the last step and walked forward to stand before the doors. He removed a glove and ran his hand across the face. "Ironwood," he said. "Black as night and tough as any metal. Fae change lovers the way humans change clothes. The Black Queen could have continued a relationship with Oberon. No offense, my Queen," he quickly added.

"None taken, Hunter," she answered. "There was a time such a statement would have seemed hurtful, but I have lived a long time among the Fae. Perhaps some are faithful for all time, but all time is an extremely long time."

"She might have shared the King," Cahal said, joining the centaur, facing the fourteen-foot-high double doors made of unbreakable wood. "She could not share the title. Impressive work," he said to the taller Fae.

"Probably a foot thick," Skerrit replied. "I know brute strength will not break them down. I'm not sure if magik can force them open."

"Then let's try something simpler," Cahal said. He took hold of a large black handle. Some type of metal, but not iron or iron alloy. He twisted it clock-wise, heard a delicate click, and pulled. The right-side door swung out, making not a squeak as it pivoted on oiled hinges.

The three entered, two with swords drawn, and one with an automatic pistol in hand. Cahal closed the door. The grand entrance was familiar. The same dimensions and design as Oberon's, but with black marble. The carvings were in the same locations, and on the same scale. Where those on Earth appeared to be happy, welcoming sprites and fairies, ghouls and vampire-looking faces with extended fangs adorned the walls here.

"Baobhan sith," Skerrit said. "Fae version of vampires. Beautiful women who will drain you of your blood. They have hooves instead of feet, and fast as any deer. Hunted them before non-terrestrial vampires gated to Earth. Pretty sure I caught and killed every one of them."

"This could be a remembrance," Titania said. "A carving of a creature long extinct. Or she found some." Her voiced dropped when she added, "Or bred some. I imagine if a warrior goddess of the Fae mated with a non-terrestrial vampire, and added a touch of this and that in a potion, she might give birth to a baobhan sith."

"You believe the Black Queen is mothering some of her Un-Seelie?" Cahal asked.

"Mothering? No," the Queen responded. "Birthing? I have no doubt," she added.

"Well, I hope she has better taste than to bed something that would result in a ghoul this ugly," Skerrit said, examining another carving.

"Ideas on where she would keep Sionnach?" Cahal asked.

"Dungeons," Titania and Skerrit answered in unison.

"If this is a true replica, there will be dungeons two floors down," Titania said.

Skerrit said. "Four lower levels total. Each level down becomes more pitiful. Cells are smaller, damper, and with less light. Quickest way down will be the back stairs from the kitchen. The way guards travel from their quarters to the dungeons. The kitchen stairwell is wider with fewer turns. The public stairwells twist and turn. They are filled with statues and carvings designed to scare the crap outta you, even if you're only visiting."

Chapter 18

The eerie quiet of the dark corridors changed to a beehive of activity when Titania opened the door to the main kitchen. Brownies, fairies, and an assortment of beings unfamiliar to her worked preparing enough food for a battalion.

The three entered and stood to the side, waiting for some reaction to their presence. A portly creature in black apron over green coveralls made its way through the hubbub toward them. Brows lowered, and eyes squinting, it moved gracefully through and around creatures, tables, and assorted carts on wheels.

"If the Queen expects me to be feeding her guests while trying to prepare a meal for after her pretend battle, I do not have the time," it warned them, meaty fists on hips, and chin thrust forward.

"We would never presume to place an undue burden on her chef," Cahal said. "You will have a lot of hungry troops to feed shortly."

"Aye, two-thousand-six-hundred-twelve, plus the Queen and her guard," the kitchen master replied.

"Plus three," he added. Assuming it a he, from the baritone voice and stubbled face and chin.

"I recognize some of the Fae on your staff, but there are some I do not know," Cahal continued.

"Nor do I recognize you," the kitchen master said, eyes narrowing.

"We're hybrids," he answered easily. "We do not fit any particular category. We are also warriors. Killing things we do not recognize is not unusual," he warned. Considering Pandaemonium was home to the UnSeelie, it seemed reasonable even polite hybrid-Fae would also have a twisted side.

Cahal's calm demeanor and implied threat obliged the cook to step back and reappraise the interlopers. He gave Titania a good look. Awe overcame his distaste over the interruption of work when he realized Skerrit's size and noticed his weapons.

"No need for violence in the Queen's kitchen," he said. "My name is Twarque, and I am not a Fae, or hybrid, or from this dimension. I was brought here to cook for the Queen. She could not find or design anything capable of preparing an edible meal. Some of my staff are also aliens. Some are the Queen's Folk, but their breeding made them unsuitable for battle. Timid. Good workers. Not fighters like you. Would you like me to prepare something for you?"

The initial complaint regarding any special privilege forgotten.

"No, Twarque. You have too much work, and the meal must be ready by . . . "

Twarque turned to look at a row of hourglasses on a mantle.

"Four-hours and a bit," he replied.

Sand was nearly three-quarters into the lower holder on one timer. Six to its left, the bottoms filled; four to the right the same way. These would be turned as sand emptied from a neighbor.

"The Queen commanded us to review security for her dungeons," Cahal whispered to Twarque. "She expects a great deal more use in the coming days. We will eat when the others arrive."

"Of course. Do I need to show you the way?"

"We know the way," Cahal assured him. Best they appeared comfortable and in control. The less suspicious the kitchen master, the less likely he might leave his tasks to find confirmation.

Titania led, with Skerrit close behind. Cahal hesitated long enough to whisper again. "After a long day on the battlefield, even if it is only practice, the Queen and her troops will be hungry and tired. I suggest you plan on more food than you think, and have it waiting for their arrival. The dungeons will be busy enough without filling them early."

As he followed the other two through a doorway on the far side of the large kitchen, a smile arose as he heard Twarque exhort his staff to greater speed, and to collect more supplies from storage.

"Well done," Titania said after the door shut. "The perfect mix of gentleman and murderer. The cook will be too busy for the next four hours to give us another thought."

"I suppose being Dúnmharú is nearer UnSeelie than Seelie," he responded. "Light soul and dark soul. Gentleman and murderer. We need to find Sionnach and get off this plane in less than four hours."

"Let's hope the Queen and her army don't come home by the same road we came in on," the centaur added.

From the landing to the kitchen, they went down. The first sub-level was used for storage, with extra rooms to house workers and soldiers. Twelve more steps down and they reached a turn-about. They descended another twelve steps to the first dungeon level.

A quartz-like crystal provided enough light to navigate the stairs. Similar to the Fae moonstones, it brightened as they neared and dimmed as they moved on.

A corridor, lit by more of the crystals, disappeared into darkness. Cells lined the right side as far as they could see.

Titania held her hand up for silence. A few seconds later she said, "I cannot hear anything breathing."

"I don't smell anything fresh or living," the Hunter added. "I think this level is empty."

They continued down, thirteen steps and thirteen more, to the next level. They all heard noise coming from a cell down the hallway. Weapons drawn, they proceeded with Titania leading and her side to the left wall. Cahal next, walking the right side, checking each cell before motioning Titania to continue forward. Skerrit watched their backs and the corridor behind them. His bow held an arrow notched and ready to fly.

Titania pointed at the fifth cell, indicating to Cahal it was not empty. The Dúnmharú pulled his blue blade with his left hand, keeping the 9-mm pistol up and ready with his right.

A figure sat on the dirt and stone floor. Tattered green dress flowed around her body. Red hair, once full and wavy, hung heavy, covering her face. She hummed and drew symbols in the dirt.

Titania stood beside Cahal, pulled closer by the familiar tune the captive female hummed.

"Epona," she whispered. "Epona, it is Queen Titania."

A porcelain face lifted. Large round eyes, brown and sad appraised the pair beyond the bars.

"She found our refuge," the Fae Royal from the past said. "My horses fought until all were killed." The symbol in the dirt was an outline of a horse's head and neck. "The Yeth Hounds would have all died as well, but the Black Queen held me. She placed a blade at my neck and ordered them to obey her or watch me die. I have not seen them since coming to this foul place."

"We will free you, Epona," Titania told the beaten goddess. "We've seen your hounds, and they are well."

"Nothing is well in Pandaemonium," she responded. "She attempted to breed me to things I cannot describe. I knew her. We were friends. What she is now I cannot say. The bars are iron. I cannot escape. I tried."

Epona held her palms up. The faint illumination provided by the quartz was sufficient to show the scars of burns and scalding.

"The iron will not hurt us," Titania told her. "We will get you out and take you home."

"Do so on your way out," the red-headed woman with the eyes of a colt said. "You must fetch Sionnach Catharnagh first. He is held on the next level. The Black Queen expects a rescue attempt. He is bound by chains and magic. He is guarded by murder and ferocity."

Skerrit joined the others, a profound sadness pulling his wide shoulders to the ground.

"I am sorry to see one who is a friend to all animals, and the patron to horses, treated such," he said to the woman on the floor. "Epona and Centaurs have been allies closer than relatives since the time of the first Folk awakening. We will come back and free you, dear friend. Together we will avenge your horses."

Epona gave him a single nod of her head before lowering it and returning to her finger pictures.

"Murder and ferocity," Skerrit repeated Epona's warning as they retraced their steps back to the stairwell.

"Don't forget chains and magic," Titania said, taking the lead as they headed down.

They stopped before stepping into the corridor. Cahal dropped to the floor and peeked around the corner.

"Can't tell how many, but a group is mucking about down the hallway. Fifty or sixty yards," he said.

"I smell something further down," Skerrit said. "The group you saw reeks of body odor and alcohol, but something more foul waits in the pitch."

"We don't have time to waste," Titania said. "Whatever creatures guard Sionnach, we must confront them."

"Agreed," Cahal said. "But we can use surprise to improve the odds. Queen Titania, may I borrow your helmet?"

Chapter 19

"Thank you," Campbell said.

Annabeth did not respond. She held a hand out to help lift the man from the floor.

"Michele?"

"On our way," Quan answered Annabeth's call. "Tom Farway and James McWaters are both dead."

When the tall Eurasian reached her new boss, Campbell, Simone Sinclair, Camila Raoul, and Kristy Nichol were with her.

"There is a security agent covering the hotel bar, one in the basement of the mall, and Toole is covering the restaurant. What we have is you, me, Simone, Kristy, Campbell, and Daegen."

"Maggie, you there?" Annabeth asked.

"Always," the reply.

"Contact the FBI Special Agent and tell him levels one and two are cleared. Have them send reinforcements, and make sure they know who and where we have security agents stationed. When we hit the third level, they need to be prepared to handle anyone or anything trying to escape."

"Sommers, you still at the bar?"

"Roger."

"Join Franco in the mall basement. Franco, you copy?"

"Loud and clear," he called back.

"When Sommers reaches you, the two of you move up and cover the North escalators and stairwells. Atlanta PD and FBI will join you."

"Copy."

"Toole?"

"Yes, ma'am."

"Same thing on the South end. Your job is to make sure nothing escapes. Vampires and thralls move fast, people. If you ask them to surrender, you're opening yourself up. Anything trying to get out is to be met with deadly force. Overwhelming deadly force."

Three 'copies' answered.

"Maggie, make sure you pass that along to the people in charge outside," Annabeth ordered.

"Without power, we don't have intel on how many we face or where they may be placed," she warned her team. "We think the dhampir are in the fitness center, but it's old info."

"I do have some new intel," Maggie interrupted. "The architect is in Europe. The offices were operating with a couple of secretaries and interns. The App developer uses off-site code-writers. No more than two or three people actually in the office. The law offices would have had the most people. The gym shows a scheduled class, but no idea how many people would have joined."

"Thanks, Maggie," the Overlord of Atlanta replied.

"Six of us," Michele said. "Four vampires left, probably eight dhampir, and let's estimate a dozen mixed thralls and human servants. Maybe we should wait on the local LEOs."

"Hate to interrupt again," Maggie said into everyone's ear. "Diego Haas is live, or, I guess, undead on the internet. He has a battery-powered camera, he's set up a hotspot using his smart phone, and they have LED lighting. Wait. Okay, they have two cameras going. He's promising to give the world a demonstration of what vampires are capable of accomplishing. From the backgrounds, I'd say one camera in the law offices and one in the gym."

"Michele, you have to get into the gym. Dhampirs are uncontrollable. If they are released, the women inside will be slaughtered. Take Kristy, Raoul, and Campbell. Simone, you go, too. Whatever witchcraft you have, protect our people and save those women."

"You?" Simone asked.

"I'm the new Overlord," Annabeth answered. "I'm going to show Hass, and the other assholes who want to make vampires look like terrorists, I am more than a title."

"Alone?" Kristy asked.

"Dae. You're with me, Buddy. Watch my back."

The black shepherd ghosted away from his sentry position to sit beside the red-headed vampire.

"Maggie, keep everyone else off the third floor. We aren't going to have the luxury of waiting to identify good guys with guns. Let's go."

Annabeth sped away toward the South end of the mall. Quan checked her magazines, pointed at Simone to follow her, followed by Kristy, then Camila, with Campbell on rear.

"I feel like the manager of an all-girl band," the only male left in the fight said to himself, waiting for Raoul to cover several non-moving escalator steps before moving.

Nearing the top of the escalator steps, the side walls turned to plexiglass. Quan slowed and dropped into a crouch. Instead of popping up, she lifted the scope off of her FN automatic rifle and held it up, turned to scan the corridor. A quick flip of a switch and she received the video from the combination scope and camera inside the night-vision goggles.

She spoke softly. She knew her words would be easily heard by everyone on the team, as well as Annabeth and Maggie. No reason to broadcast their location to anyone else.

"I counted eight bad guys with at least a dozen hostages spread out along both sides of the corridor. The hostages are tied up and seated on the floor away from the walls. The entrance to the gym is at the top of the escalator, right, and less than ten feet. Double glass doors. No guards and no movement behind the glass."

"No way we can take out eight shooters without collateral damage," Raoul whispered. "How many innocents are we willing to lose to save the majority?"

"None," Simone answered. "Not so long as a Legacy has a say. I can handle the guards in the hallway. I will need someone to help free the hostages."

"Raoul, you are with Simone," Quan ordered. "Kristy is with me. We're going to hit the gym as soon as Simone makes her play. James, you have to watch our backs. From the top you will have eyes on the corridor, the gym, and the escalator. Simone, it's your move."

The modern Legacy Witches are not as powerful as the original twelve. Twenty-five-thousand-years of wear, missed generations, fewer responsibilities, and the simple drain of magic meant weaker witches. But a weak Legacy Witch was stronger than any other human magical manipulator. Spell Casters, for instance, needed to speak an incantation aloud. They also required a focus item to assure the spell reached a specific target. They could not control an element.

Simone Sinclair controlled air. She could preform many magical acts, but calling air to her aid overshadowed all other talents. A Legacy could cast a spell silently, and, while a focus helped, it was not required. Especially not in a closed area such as the third floor of a downtown shopping mall.

The willowy blonde centered herself, preparing the air around her to heed her command. She raised her hands and walked up the final few metal steps, Camila Raoul behind her, remained crouched and, hopefully, out of sight.

"I have come to speak with the vampire in charge," she called before a nervous finger pulled a delicate trigger. "The Council of Four is prepared to negotiate the release of Arina Kishka."

As she called out her lie, she psychically framed her spell, telling the air to disperse from the hallway. Ordering the oxygen to move away from the people in the corridor.

Her announcement created a wave of discussions. These were low-end human servants. They had no authority to do anything but guard and kill. The lowering of oxygen to their brains made it no easier to decide if they should call their leader.

In near harmony, the eight felt their vision blur, their balance desert them, and the hard floor rise up to catch their oxygen-deprived bodies. Moments later, the hostages followed. With their lungs closer to the ground, it took a few seconds longer before their blood stopped delivering the needed element to their brains.

"Take a deep breath and hurry," Simone told Raoul. "We have to pull the hostages into the architect offices."

Following her own instructions, the witch took a deep breath and hurried to the first body tied with plastic pull-ties. She and Raoul could take fresh air after pulling each hostage into the offices. But they had to act quickly to prevent anyone from suffering brain damage.

Behind the witch and security agent, Quan and Nichol rushed out of the escalator housing. Quan fired a burst at the right-side door, shattering the safety glass and making a hole for her to pass through. There was no time to determine if the doors were locked or open.

The two women rushed past a reception desk, and through a privacy door, which swung inward, after the Eurasian led with her shoulder.

The interior studio was lit with LED lights on tripods. A digital camera also sat on a three-legged stand, pointed at a row of women, Like the hostages in the corridor, all were bound at the wrists and ankles with pull-ties.

Unlike the guards outside, the four manning the camera and guarding the women had plenty of oxygen. Two moved incredibly fast, closing on Quan before Nichol cleared the doorway.

"Thrall," Michele said aloud. Six years as a Council of Four special security agent meant six years of dealing with witches, Fae, and vampires. With vampires came human servants who wanted to become more than human. The first step to becoming a terrestrial vampire was to reach a position of trust where a vampire allowed their blood to be taken to replace blood given. Following the exchange, the person became something more than human, but not equal to a full vampire.

Something more came with an extended lifespan, strength, and speed.

Michele Quan had her own brand of speed. It came with practice and enhanced by adrenaline.

She employed an aikido block and body roll to send her first attacker sailing. The female's arms flailed before momentum slammed her into a brick wall. Quan continued the roll. She pivoted and dropped low so the fist swung by the second thrall, a male, passed over her head. When his eyes lowered to find her new level, he looked into the business end of the FN. Thralls are fast. Bullets are faster.

A dozen 5.56-mm steel-jacketed projectiles turned the vampire-wannabe's head to shattered bone, skin, grey membrane, and pink fluids.

Kristy Nichol engaged the two human servants. One pulled a friction knife and stood between the pilot and the hostages. The second ran toward his own reflection and long guns stacked against a studio mirror.

With her left hand, she raked bullets in a tight figure-eight at the human trying for the rifles. On full automatic and with the sweeping pattern, she did not aim, but trusted some of the slugs would find the mark.

The suppressed FN was quiet enough for the unique sound of a bullet piercing skin to be heard, followed quickly by raspy groans and the sound of shattered mirror falling onto an expensive teak workout floor.

The thrall who launched herself at Quan pushed away from the wall, turning to continue the attack. She turned to discover the pretty asian-looking woman with the funny goggles already there. Over thee-hundred years old, the woman had attacked more than a few people in those centuries. In every instance they either froze or tried to escape. The heroic ones stood their ground, or gave a few steps as they attempted to extend their lifetime. Never had someone pressed their own attack.

As an elite security agent, Quan received training in all styles of personal combat. With her experience, she opted to carry one specific combat knife. The SOG Fixation Bowie. The seven-inch blade was well balanced and sharp. The Kraton wrap-around checkered handle fit her hand perfectly. It was not the most versatile military-style knife. It did one thing, and it did it well.

The blade slashed deeply into the thrall's exposed throat, cutting to the spine, and siding across the skin, muscle and tendons like butter. The only disadvantage to close quarters combat was the spray of fluids caught her full-face. Thankfully the night-vision goggles kept the liquid out of her eyes. She kept her mouth tightly closed.

Kristy switched the FN to single fire and leveled the futuristic-looking compact rifle at the man with the folding knife, most likely picked up from a local home repair super store.

He dropped the weapon and went to his knees, hands intertwined behind his head.

"Done this before, have you," she said, placing the muzzle of the rifle on the top of his head and sending him down until his forehead rested on the wood floor.

"Don't move in front of the camera," Quan said to her, having ghosted across the dance floor. "Look to your left."

Kristy turned and saw the eight crates set side-by-side against a far wall. They were plated metal with wide metal bands securing them. Double locks held the bands firmly together atop the crates.

"Are those charges attached to the locks?" Kristy asked.

"That would be my guess," Quan confirmed. "Remote detonation. If the camera is on the hostages, and we try to move them, whoever is watching will blast those locks."

"And whatever is inside will be outside," Nichol finished.

"Maggie?" Michele said.

"I've been listening," the tech answered. "The vampires have two live feeds on the internet. No audio, and the video isn't the best. One is the law offices and shows a bunch of people bound and seated on the floor. The other shows the women in the gym. The gym stream is getting the most comments. Four of the hostages had their tops taken or cut off by the assholes. You can imagine the stupid tits and nipple comments being added."

Kristy kicked the bad guy in the ribs. She kicked him hard. When he curled into a fetal position, plastic ties fell from his jacket's pocket. She used the ties to bind his hands and feet. She forced him onto his stomach and connected hands to feet with another plastic tie.

"Maggie, can you tape the video and hack the feed?" Michele asked.

"Loop the tape so people watching continue to see women helplessly tied up on the floor," she said back. "I'm looking for a way to hack the signal while the tape is running."

A long minute passed, and then they received the answer. "Signal is being broadcast through a modem in the law offices on back-up battery. I looped the video of the gym. You should have a little time before someone notices the same movements and positions keep repeating."

Michele pulled her Bowie and Kristy collected the friction blade off the floor. They hastened to cut ties and get the women out and down the stairs before someone blew open the crates.

Annabeth heard Simone and Camilla report they were barricaded inside the architectural firm's office with the hostages from the corridor. Simone had kept the air away for a long time. The coterie members in the hallway were dead or suffered irreparable brain damage.

Michele and Kristy herded fitness studio members and staff down the escalator steps. Police and Feds were given a heads-up by Maggie. They waited at the bottom level to take the women out. The hostages from the restaurant, and a three store workers found hiding in closed shops had already been escorted away from the mall.

Michele, Kristy, and James waited beside the escalator housing, keeping watch on the shattered entrance to the gym. If any loud bangs occurred, they needed to be prepared to take down dhampirs trying to leave the gym. They would not be able to see the entrance to the law offices at the far end of the corridor with or without night-vision.

Annabeth rubbed Dae's neck and gave the dog a loving scratch between his ears.

"Time," she said, standing.

Chapter 20

"The Queen has returned. How is the prisoner?" Cahal called as he walked toward the group. He placed as much authority in his stride as he could muster. He also gave full control to his dark soul; his Fae.

He wore Titania's blood-red leather helmet and had Fin's fine white cloak wrapped around his right hand. It billowed free from his left side, exposing the Cerrullan blade hanging from his waist.

"And who the lick-my-nuts are you?" one of the group asked, moving forward and taking command. He wore dirty clothes, if smell meant anything. He needed a shave, and hid stringy hair beneath a bright red tam.

"I am Cahal Kearney, the Dúnmharú," he answered truthfully. "I am the Royal Executioner, the Queen's Assassin, the man who murders Fae and non-Fae without fear of recourse. The one who will place your balls in a glass jar so you never need worry again about getting them licked."

He stopped two yards from the red-cap. The group, near enough now to see as units, consisted of a total of five, including the scrawny, hawk-nosed red-cap. The other four appeared to be all males. No two alike, but all the same. The type of low-lifes who would follow anyone who promised profits and the opportunity to inflict pain.

"Never heard of you, Dumb Mary Lou," the leader squawked, laughing at his play on Kearney's title. "Any time the Black Queen wants me, she sends her little Leanne. The bitch what enjoys hurting others more than myself."

"Hurting others is my job," Cahal said. "The Queen sent me for a simple answer. You have already wasted my time with your stupidity. I will ask once more, how is the prisoner?"

"The same," the red-cap replied. "He don't talk. He don't beg. We used him as a target, but his skin don't break. We've raped and butchered women, men, and children in front of him to get him to answer my questions. He's let them all die without a peep. He may be a Seelie son-of-a-bitch, but he's got balls. Tried to cut one off, but my knife wouldn't bite. There's your answer for the Queen, Dumb Mary Lou. The prisoner is a pain in my ass. I'd kill him dead if I could find a way."

"You raped and murdered men, women, and children to try and break him?" Cahal asked.

"Aliens, half-breeds without enough hatred to make them worth a spit, and one tasty meadow fairy I'd had my eye on for a while," red-cap replied. "We'd have done 'em anyway. This way it was at the Queen's request. I like getting paid for pleasure."

Cahal released his grip on the cape. The same hand holding the folded cloth also held a 9-mm Gloch with a chambered round. The bullet tore a path through the red-cap's forehead, blasting a crater as it exited the rear of his skull. The dumbfounded look on the UnSeelie quickly replaced by a blank death-stare as his body fell. The Dúnmharú continued pulling the trigger, firing the twelve remaining cartridges into the four henchmen. All head shots, taking no chance on wounding any of the murderers.

He turned his attention to the cell. A man sat on a stone stool built into the stone wall. He wore torn leather britches and nothing else. Dark damp hair hung down to cover his forehead; face tilted down.

"If your idea is to rescue me and escape through a horde of the Black Queen's vermin, I have to give you credit for the entrance. Killing those bastards is a nice touch. But I'm not leading you back to Earth," the man said, not bothering to look up.

"Don't need directions," Cahal answered. "I have my own. Oberon gave them to me before I left."

Dark eyes lifted. A strong face, a bit gaunt, but still handsome gazed up at Cahal.

"If you were sent by Oberon, then we have one problem, and you have another," he said.

Cahal stood waiting. Sionnach may be half-human, but Fae have a way of extending conversations needlessly. If you want them to get to a point, it's best to shut up. Let his half-Fae side fill in the void.

"The iron bars do not affect me," he said. "There is a ward to keep the cell door closed."

"You wear a silver ring on your left hand," the Dúnmharú said. "I was told you know how to use it to open warded plane gates. Why not use it on the cell door?"

"My mother gave me this ring," Sionnach answered. "She said it would enhance the magic I inherited from her side of the family. Since I am a male, I could not call on magic the way my female relatives could. It isn't strong enough to displace the Black Queen's magic. But your problem is about to make my escape mute."

The captured warrior pointed to his right, directing Cahal's attention to his left, and down the shadowed corridor of dungeon keeps.

A blackness moved in the darkness. A lumbering wall of ebon moving from the gloom toward the light. Toward Cahal.

"My real guard," Sionnach said. "Caileach's Tophet Hound."

The animal appeared. It had the head and body shape of a Rottweiler, but stood six-feet tall at its shoulders. With the body partially obscured by the shadowing, Cahal still guessed it weighed close to a small horse. The eyes blazed red and yellow, the color of the flames in the Valley of Hinnon.

If the Red-cap represented Epona's reference to murder, the Tophet Hound was the ferocity preventing the Black Queen's prize from escaping.

"You think you can deal with that?" Sionnach asked.

"Not my problem," Cahal answered. His turn; he pointed to his right. The prisoner needed to stand and lean forward to see down the corridor.

Skerrit, in his true form, a huge roan-colored body of a stallion, his naked, heavily muscled torso and arms rising above the withers, charged down the hallway. On the back of the centaur rode Titania with gladius in hand.

The Fae's legendary hunter released a half-dozen arrows as he neared. Cahal moved closer to Sionnach's barred cell, turning to watch as the head of each shaft impacted.

Those hitting the Hound's head bounced off. The three aimed at his chest and shoulders pierced the black hair cover. The creature yelled, a sound of anger. Huge teeth appeared, and claws of a lion emerged from its paws.

Sparks flew from the stone floor as Skerrit's steel-clad hooves dug into the surface. The Centaur and Titan rushed past. The stallion plowed into the hound, sending the huge canine skittering backward. Skerrit used his hooves to strike at the dog's face. The iron-alloy shoes cutting half-moon dents in the Tophet Hound's muzzle and cheeks.

Titania dropped lightly from the centaur's shoulders, her blade, also steel, slicing into the hound's paws, sheering claws to prevent it from ripping into Skerrit.

The bellows released by the injured beast rocked the dungeon. Stone dust rained down and iron bars rang in sympathy.

Skerrit, his own sword in hand, used the advantage of his height to slash down at the UnSeelie creature. Titania, having declawed the front paws, stabbed up into the animal's exposed neck. Fetid ichor ran freely from its wounds.

The hound tried to rise up to bite the centaur. Its damaged front feet slipped on its body fluids, now pooling on the dungeon floor. The huge head slammed to the ground between splayed front legs.

Titania used the advantage to hack into the hound's neck. Skerrit moved sideways, and used his longer blade to slice across the gash Titania opened. Twice more they took turns at the growing wound. The head separated from the body. The body collapsed.

The odor from the severed neck made all of them clutch, fighting back vomit. The smell of sacrificed children and burning garbage. The smell of Tophet.

"Skerrit! Titania!" Sionnach called. "What a sight. What a battle. Did you have to open the dog up? The ward on this cell keeps me in, but does not keep smells out."

Skerrit retained his horse-form, trotting over to stand in front of the small cell. He needed to twist and bend to see inside the prison chamber.

"A compliment followed by a complaint," he said. "I guess we arrived before the Black Queen could beat that trait out of you."

"Glad to see you still live," Titania said, joining them, her sword in hand. "Can we get you out now?"

"I don't see how," the prisoner answered. "I'm sure the magic used in the ward is stronger than brute strength. The ward surrounds the cell walls, not only the doorway. I tried breaking through the stone. It's all covered."

"Cahal?" Titania asked.

"Cahal Kierney," Sionnach said. "It's what you called yourself when you marched down the hall. The Dark Descendant of Catharnagh."

"He's the pup you left at Oberon's castle over two decade gone," Skerrit said. "He's your son."

The two men stood. Each taking the measure of the other.

"A miracle, Queen Titania. Two Catharnaghs quiet at the same time," Skerrit joked. "But someone needs to say something. All of this noise may bring guards, and the Black Queen is still on her way."

A glimmering dust devil began forming at the centaur's hooves. The magic would turn him from horse to humanoid in a few seconds.

As Skerrit transformed and Titania sheathed her weapon, Cahal raised his left hand and spoke to his sire.

"Bishop placed this ring on my finger when I was thirteen. Like yours, it was created by Legacy magic. Unlike yours, mine was spelled to contain wild magic. Magic I inherited when my mother and sister both died."

Sionnach did not respond. Damiana Sinclair gave birth to Cahal prematurely. He had been off-world with Oberon, not expecting the early arrival caused by a frantic, unplanned plane trip from Quebec to Paris. The pilot made an emergency landing in Ireland when Dammie began bleeding. She died of blood loss without ever seeing her newborn son or stillborn daughter. Sionnach experienced the sadness tinged with shame he felt every time he thought of his deceased love.

Cahal placed his left palm against the cell door, making contact between the silver ring and the ward. He waited.

Sionnach took a moment, then realized what his son wanted. He placed his left palm against Cahal's, the magical barrier between them.

The Dúnmharú nodded, and spoke the spell he was taught to use to open dimensional portals closed off by magic. Sionnach used the same incantation. As their words merged, the entire cell began to glow in a soft blue light. At the last syllable, their hands touched, their fingers locked. The ward had fallen.

Chapter 21

"If the cook is right, we have less than three hours before the Black Queen and her army arrive," Titania said.

"This won't take long," Skerrit promised.

With Cahal and Sionnach on either side, the three pulled the door from its hinges. Epona remained where she sat.

"I am too tired to flee and too worn to fight," she said. "You must hurry. Leave."

Skerrit, gentler than any might believe the big being to be, lifted the Fae. He pushed damp red hair from her face, smiled at her, and said, "You're part of the herd. You know what that means."

"We stay together," she answered. Her small smile cracked a dirty face and lit her large brown eyes. A light rekindled in the Princess of Ponies.

As they raced through the busy kitchen, Skerrit leading to make sure no one slowed them, Epona's hand gripped in his, the others grabbed anything that looked edible. Sionnach and Epona needed food for energy sapped by the dungeons.

"That place made me feel old and beaten," the rescued Fae warrior told Titania as they rushed down a long corridor. "I was there a few days. Epona has been captive for untold years. She's stronger than I realized."

"There is a reason horses and dogs are drawn to Epona," Titania replied. "Not because she has sworn to protect them with her life, but because she embodies the best qualities of both. She will toil until she drops, race until she wins, run until she cannot stand, and gives her love without condition. She is loyal and true. She was the best of the Seelie."

"She will be again," Sionnach swore.

They exited through the huge ironwood doors, the yellow-red sun of Pandaemonium low on the horizon facing them.

On the steps of the black castle Skerrit fed Epona grains and fruits. Cahal grabbed a skin-bag of fresh water as he raced through the kitchen. He passed this to the Fae, who thanked him with her smile. After two long pulls, she poured a handful and washed grime from her face. Feeling better, she handed the skin to Sionnach. The Fae-Human finished his stolen bread smeared with a jam-like substance. The water helped revive his spirit as well.

A glitter dust-devil rose around the Hunter turning him back into a Centaur. He held his hand for Epona, who seemed to weigh nothing as he lifted her to his wide back.

"The exit gate is less than one-hundred-yards from the entry portal," Titania said. "A straight road before us."

The return trip would go much faster than the cautious journey to the black castle. Titania, Sionnach, and Cahal possessed amazing speed and could outdistance the four-legged centaur if they wished.

Skerrit galloped away, Epona at ease on his back. Titania kept pace off his front right shoulder. Cahal and Sionnach ran behind and on either side of the big rump.

The newly acquainted father and son remained quiet as they ran. Both conflicted by their relationship and the chasm between them. Sionnach turned his young son over to the Fae to raise. There would be questions as to why, and why he chose to stay out of Cahal's life. Cahal spent years questioning people as to who his father was, discovering the truth only recently from his grandmother, Simone Sinclair. At the moment he could not think of anything to say to the half-human, half-Fae who sired him.

The myriad thoughts and feelings coursing through the two men ended abruptly as Titania and Skerrit halted.

"The sky ahead," she said.

Dark-winged birds circled. Crows or some Pandaemonium version of carrion bird.

"They're over the bridge where I knocked out the trolls," Skerrit said.

"Titania will see them and send UnSeelie to investigate," the Queen said. "We must go faster."

They did. Skerrit at a full run and the other three matching his speed. When they reached the bridge birds scattered, disturbed from tearing at the two huge corpses.

Cahal quickly evaluated the situation, trained by the Council of Four's security experts in crime scene investigation.

"They killed one another," he said. "Probably blamed each other for letting us escape."

"Here they come," Sionnach said. He pointed to the South. Across the desolate brown landscape a dust cloud rose and moved in their direction. "Go," he called.

Once more at speed, the five fled for the foothills where the portal waited.

The daughter of the Black Queen rode at the front. Her mother saw the crozzards circling beyond the castle. More curious than concerned, she dispatched Leanne Shee to discover what carrion attracted the swarm.

Leanne, born of the Queen and a vampire from the Cerrul dimension, knew better than to question her mother's orders. Such imperious actions stripped from her as a child. The dungeons made a lasting impression.

She mounted her phooka, a horse-like beast with a nasty temperament and long, jagged teeth. She used a chain for reins to control the wild animal. Phooka were not her favorite mode of transport, but they were fast and could run at top speed for hours in the heat of the desolate world.

Her personal guard of six dark elf hybrids took up positions behind her. They provided protection, a source of blood, and helped slake her sexual appetite. She inherited all the base instincts and desires of her mother and father. Any potential from traits not associated with cruelty beaten from her at a young age.

The athletic woman rode the phooka like a jockey. Long black hair in the wind, and strong hands with long red nails wrapped around the chains used to guide the steed. Her head thrust forward and low, she complained to the beast as they raced over baked soil.

"Hours from home," she said, her teeth clenched, the words a snarl. "A bath, fresh clothes, or better, no clothes. Sucking on fresh blood. Or fresh men. I am sick of dirt and grit in my mouth."

She wore a leather vest, tied across the chest with leather strings. The lacing left sufficient space for her breasts to be admired. A billowing skirt of black lace allowed her to ride with bare thighs melding her to the equine. Black knee boots dangled as she preferred riding without a saddle. It did not prevent her from using silver spurs to goad the wild beast to greater speed.

"Faster you bastard," she said. "Get this over quickly and I may not feed on you."

The Phooka's ears turned forward, and the animal's neck seem to lengthen as it quickened its pace, opening up into long strides used to gobble distance like a prairie fire in a wind.

The Dark Princess closed her coal-black eyes and pressed her red lips firmly shut. She let her body take control while she let her mind fly free. She hated everything about her life, this world, and her destiny. Moments of absolute freedom were rare, and the wild race across the barren land provided one.

Her eyes opened when she felt the Phooka drop into the gully without losing speed. The sudden shift in elevation did not cause her to lose her seat, nor did the fast climb up the far side onto the Road to Air and Darkness.

She turned her mount toward Air, the foothills and the portals; away from Darkness, her mother's castle. They continued down the road until she pulled hard on the chains, cutting the silver bit into the phooka's mouth. She forced the beast to a sliding stop as it approached the Styx bridge.

She slid from the animal's back. She stood examining the two massive bodies when her guard caught up. The crozzards, massive black-winged carrion-eaters, soared away as she approached. Some took to the sky, and some simply flew a short distance and settled on the roadway, waiting for their meal to be returned.

"The idiots killed each other," she said to Donagh, the guard captain. He stood at the edge of the bridge, the chains to his phooka in hand. "You are not much use as guards if you cannot keep up," she told him. "I may need to find better riders or faster animals."

"Princess Leanne," Keara, a female with dark black skin, called out from her mount. She pointed toward Air. "Dust. Someone is running in that direction. Perhaps they saw what happened."

She turned, caught sight of dust rising from the roadway, and whistled. Her steed rushed ahead, parting the guard and nearly running over the captain. It did not slow as it passed her. She grabbed the chains and jumped onto the animal's back, the sword and scabbard on her hip slapping the phooka's flank like a riding whip.

The hybrids hurried to catch their liege, the captain scurrying to mount his own ride and catch the guard. His time as the head of the Princess's babysitters would soon be over if he did not reach them before they reached those responsible for the dust.

Chapter 22

Annabeth sent Dae into the shadows of a nook beside the entry to the law offices. She moved toward the open doors. The interior lit by portable LED lights revealed the cluster of hostages seated on the floor behind the reception island. Unlike the women in the gym, these people were not tied. The presence of four terrestrial vampires, five thralls, and four human servants enough to quell thoughts of escape.

She stood at the threshold taking in everything the way a seasoned military operator would. The layout was simple. An island-style reception desk where two people would normally handle incoming calls and visitors. Two chairs placed along the short wall to her left. Same for the wall to her right. The walls ended in doors that provided access to the firm's law offices, conference rooms, and such. A person would need a card with magnetic strip to enter, or be buzzed through by the receptionist.

A longer wall behind the desk held pictures of partners. Twenty-seven people sat on their butts beneath the portraits. Three hostages with likenesses in oil above them. Partners. Now equal to every other person on the staff.

Ché, a female vampire nearly twenty-five-hundred-years old sat in the second chair to Annabeth's left. Her dark hair and red skin traits of her Native American heritage. The pale shade of her skin testament to the length of time away from sunlight.

To Annabeth's right, a thrall sat in the first seat, an AK-47 across his lap. Next to him sat Bada Pesquero, the first vampire turned by Diego Hass, who was Arina's first turn. Bada's origins were pre-Olmec. Born seven-thousand-years earlier in what is now Belize. A long curved sword of cavalry design protruded forward. Its tip settled on the tile floor. His wild hair and bushy facial hair did not go well with the two-thousand-dollar three-piece suit, or the Italian loafers.

His sire, Diego Haas stood behind the front counter of the reception island. The eldest of the lieutenants, he received control of the area from Texas to Panama under Arina. The handsome man originated from a section of South America now within Peru. His eyes, a dark golden brown, were slanted like an oriental's. Short at five-five, and slight, he made up for a lack of stature with a personality described as a cross between ferocious and tenacious. Another human servant sat to Haas' left. She could not see what either man carried for weaponry, but knew they both were armed.

A tripod stood behind the desk, the lens of a digital camera trained on the hostages. A human stood beside the camera, eyes darting between Annabeth at the doorway and a smart phone in her hand. Four thralls stood between the reception desk and the people on the floor. All carried long guns. All wore sidearms.

Leaning against the closed door to the business section on Annabeth's right, wearing a white pant suit with a lot of exposed cleavage, three-inch heel boots, and unsheathed double-edged sword in her right hand, lazed Wesa "The Cat" Sherman. No one was exactly sure of her beginnings. She was turned by Arina four-thousand-years in the past and rumored to be her favorite lieutenant. The fact Kishka meant cat, and Wesa was nicknamed "The Cat," added credence to their relationship.

Wesa's deep purple hair color with matching lip gloss and eye shadow made her pale skin glow. With the white suit, the shadows created by LED lighting against her boobs deepened the cleavage displayed by the gaping top.

Two humans, a male and a female, stood in front of the other closed door. Armed with AK-47s.

Four vamps, five thralls, and four humans. Thirteen, but unlucky for whom? How many more might wait behind those closed doors?

All of these details, plus more, observed, cataloged, and accounted for by the relatively young vampire in less than thirty-seconds.

Wearing the grey combat clothing, she was probably the worst dressed person there. Maybe the humans in their goth black, and perhaps a couple of clerks on the floor were equal to her current fashion level. She made up for her inexpensive surplus clothing with an FN-FS2000 CQB strapped across her chest. The rifle currently riding her back. Matching Sherpa thigh-holsters held Springfield AR-15 automatic pistols. Not her normal choice, but the pistols where chambered for the same 5.56-mm rounds as the

FN. The clips were not interchangeable, but in an emergency she could transfer cartridges.

The blue-metal Cerrulan sword given to her by Bishop waited in its wooden sheath belted at her waist. A dagger rested in a fore-arm sheath, and a wicked six-inch knife was Velcroed to her left calf.

You could say she was prepared for bear. Or anything else with big teeth and a bad attitude.

"I ordered you to stand down," she said. Her emerald eyes on Haas. "I only heard your decision, Diego. I will allow anyone here the chance to accept me as Overlord and leave now."

No one moved, other than hostages squirming as they realized help came in the guise of a single young woman.

"You have my regards as a warrior," Diego Haas said. "To face us alone is brave. It is stupid, but it is brave. It will not save these people, nor will the fact you are one of us save you. The world is going to see what we are capable of. Millions will witness what vampires can do to fragile humans."

"I am not one of you," Annabeth replied. "I am first-turned of Bishop. I am the only vampire sired by the eldest vampire. His blood is my blood. I offered my services to Ssara Den as a favor to an Exemplar. I did not accept his offer as Overlord to destroy members of Arina's coterie. My coterie. I came to restore faith be-tween us, the Fae, witches, and humans. Last chance. Stand down or I lose thousands of years of history, experience, and leadership with your final deaths."

"The bitch is so full of shit, I would be afraid to bite her," Ché chirped from her seat.

When outnumbered and facing a larger opponent, hide, run, or strike first.

The small Springfield pistol seemed to magically jump into her left hand. The Sherpa holster giving no resistance to her quick-draw.

Two small holes appeared in the forehead of the thrall seated on her right as she fired across her body without seeming to aim. The human next to Hass collapsed in his chair before he could lift the rifle held below the counter top. Two more 5.56-mm slugs buried in his brain.

The female camera-operator took a slug in her nape, one in her temple as she spun, and a third clipped the end of her nose. A fourth ruined the portrait of a portly partner with grey hair and aristocratic frown.

The thralls covering the hostage spun and began hosing the entrance with automatic fire. Their action, a reaction to the sudden attack, sent Hass dropping to his knees to get below the withering fire. Ché scurried away, and Bada called on vampire-reflexes to go belly down on the tile floor.

Annabeth pirouetted and changed her level, moving right. Her sword, no longer sheathed, swept across the exposed neck of the thrall she double-tapped, taking its head. Just in case.

She rolled across Bada's back. The receptionists' island covered her from the fire of the hostages' guards. Remaining low, she fired six bullets into Wesa's legs. The vampire howled as the small projectiles bit into quads, thighs, and knee caps. She would heal, but she would be off her feet for a while.

The red-headed blur tossed the empty AR-15, sheathed the blue sword, and whipped the FN from back to front like a Carnival dancer in Rio performing a seductive shimmy. The AK-47s of the thralls went silent when they realized they were wasting ammunition on an empty corridor beyond the open doors. Annabeth used the lapse to rise up and return her own rain of fire. Shooting left to right, pulling the short barrel across her body as she held the trigger closed, dozens of supersonic rounds cut through skin, clothing, bone, organs, and brains.

The hostages, cowering and gathering atop one another, were covered by red mist and ghastly body parts as the thralls disintegrated from the chest up under the withering fire.

Haas jumped up from his hole and grabbed the FN, ignoring the blistering heat of the metal muzzle. He twisted the rifle, twisting the carry-strap at the same time. The movement, combined by the raw force of his attack, spun her, locking her lower back against the island's front counter.

Bada, off the floor and face contorted by anger, grabbed her with his left hand, fingers squeezing deeply into her neck. His right hand rose, cavalry sword held out the way a rider would charge into battle. Set to decapitate anyone in his path.

Vampires, non-terrestrial or Earth-born are fast, strong, and can endure a great deal of pain. They are difficult to defeat, and nearly impossible to stop. But they remain creatures with bodies. Bodies are vulnerable, and pain is relative.

Daegen sank long white teeth into the ancient vamp's right hamstring. An average German Shepherd comes with a bite force of about two-hundred-thirty-eight pounds. Dae was above average.

The relative pain increased when the dog began shaking his head as if trying to pull the stuffing from a toy. Bada Pesquero screamed in pain unfelt and forgotten since becoming a full vampire. Pain so intense the sword fell from fingers spread wide by nerves firing off in confusion.

Dae pulled, and the vamp went back and down, face cracking loudly as it hit the tile. Bada was under a gruesome assault, but he was still a vampire with super-ordinary strength. He kicked reflexively, catching the shepherd in the chest, and sending the dog tumbling away. It freed him from the bite, but a portion of his back upper leg went with the dog.

Bada screamed and cursed in pain and panic. He rolled, pulling a .40caliber pistol from a holster hidden by his jacket. He needed a moment to stop his hand from shaking before he lined the front sight on the hated canine.

It is difficult to make your finger pull a trigger when your head is no longer attached to send the required command.

Aware of the danger she and Dae faced, Annabeth pulled the wrist-dagger and sliced through the leather strap. The sharp blade cut through her shirt and penetrated her skin to get beneath and through the tight strap. A cost she was happy to pay. As Bada readied his pistol, she swung her sword. She was faster and his head tumbled.

Haas, in spite of superior vampire reflexes, lost his balance when the strap separated. He stepped backward, holding the empty rifle. His step took him off the raised platform beneath the island.

He drew two black obsidian blades from hidden holsters. The black stone ceremonial knives his signature weapons. He stalked around the desk, passing Wesa, still writhing on the floor from the multiple gunshot wounds to her legs. Ten-thousand-years of being the ultimate predator infused him with confidence. Less than ten-minutes around Annabeth Hughes infuriated him.

The redheaded female vampire from England turned, her blue sword blade dripping attenuated blood from Bada's severed neck. Green eyes squinted, lips pinched, and her own emotions locked away. She faced the remaining coterie without anger or remorse.

Ché used her vampiric strength to toss the two humans guarding the escape door on the left toward Annabeth. The flailing bodies sailing through the air were too surprised by their idol's action to consider using their weapons.

Annabeth executed a back shoulder spin to avoid the two humans, pivoting directly into the path of the second oldest vampire in the western hemisphere; now that Arina was locked away in London.

With her one-handed sword, she blocked his first thrust. She stepped back and away from his second. Behind her Dae engaged the humans. From the shrieks of fear and agony, the dog could handle himself against both normal beings. It eased her to know the shepherd was not badly injured by Bada's kick.

Haas pressed his attack, cross slashing with both hands, aiming high, trying to damage her face, hoping to blind her.

Annabeth continued to back away. The black blades finding only air to hack. She watched the weave of Haas' hands. A normal person would see a blur of movement. For Annabeth's enhanced eyesight, it became a slow-motion hand dance. She watched, retreated, and waited. When Haas' left and right hands crossed in an x-pattern, before he could flip his palms down to lunge forward with double backhand slashes, she pulled her long sword up from the ground, rolling the sharp edge to the top. The alien blue metal sliced through the other vampire's wrists, severing his hands as a scalpel would slice through skin.

Dumbfounded, Diego Haas watched his hands fall away, obsidian blades still gripped by fingers he no longer felt. Too shocked to feel the pain, he looked at the woman in front of him with unbelieving eyes. He was a creature of death. He had wielded power for centuries, controlling cartels, downing all enemies. He believed, as Arina did, vampires would be the next gods to rule

Earth. Gods did not gush pale pink fluid from gaping forearms. Gods could not be beaten. Unless they faced something more powerful. More powerful than a god?

"What are you?" he asked.

"The Overlord," she answered, removing his head and ending his self-doubts.

On her left Ché went to her knees, tossing her leather-handled knife, and rubber-grip pistol away. She placed her hands high and said, "I recognize Annabeth Hughes as Overlord of the Southeastern Territory. I pledge my allegiance. I swear on my ancestors."

On her right, Wesa had managed to sit with her back against the wall, legs spread in front of her. "She raised a hand and said, "Same here. I recognize and I obey. Do you think I could get a painkiller, or a drink?"

Annabeth, aware the sounds of struggle no longer came from behind her, turned to see Dae standing before two bloodied humans. The male and the female holding torn arms against their chests, their rifles discarded, and their posture screaming defeat.

"I swear allegiance," the male said.

The female, unable to take her eyes from Dae's white teeth, turned a thumb up to indicate she agreed. Her voice gone from the screams caused by those fangs.

"Maggie, tell the team and inform the law they can come up and secure the hostages. Bring medics," she added.

"Will do," replied the tech.

"You know what?" Wesa said from her ass. "I think I change my mind."

She pulled a remote detonator and pressed the red button before Annabeth could reach her. The sound of sixteen small explosions rippled up from the corridor. Locks and steel bands being blasted off metal crates.

"Let's see what a bunch of crazy blood-thirsty dhampirs can do," the Cat purred.

"You will never know," Annabeth answered, bringing her blade straight down, carving a split into the vampire's skull, separating her cognitive brain from her creative brain forever.

"Maggie, warn everyone. The dhampirs in the fitness center have been released. Tell Simone to do what she can to block their exit. I need Kristy and Camila here to watch Ché, two humans, and help the hostages."

"You're all connected," Maggie answered. "Everyone heard."

Annabeth did not waste time with giving orders. As soon as Kristy and Camila ran from the gloom into the law office entry, she and Dae sped off in the direction they came from. Toward the worst possible confrontation of their lives, which included having faced Blood Dragons who spat flames and came with nearly indestructible scaled hides.

Chapter 23

Simone stood before the glass doors to the gym, palms extended as she ordered the air on this side of the entrance to compress, keeping them from opening.

"They tested the doors," she told Annabeth as the vampire arrived. "I have seen some horrid creatures in my long life, including some exceptionally ugly plane-travelers passing through on their way to other worlds. These dhampirs are the worst. I think they have been kept in those crates unfed. Dae is covered in blood."

"Not his," Annabeth replied. "We have to come up with a plan. You can't hold them in there forever. Sunrise doesn't affect them."

"Quiet," Simone ordered. She tilted her head, trying to discern some sound that wafted through her atmospheric barrier. "Did you hear anything?"

"Maybe, but I wasn't actually listening," the vampire admitted. "Maggie, can you access the video feed from inside the gym?"

"No worries," the instant response. "I've kicked the electricity back on." Then, "We have a problem, ladies. They've broken out the windows on the backside of the building. It looks like they intend to Dracula down the outside."

"Tell the police," Annabeth said. "They will have shooters watching the back alley. Tell them head shots are the only thing able to stop them." To Simone she said, "I have to go, but you can't. Unless all eight leave, this still represents a way out. Can you hold it?"

"Got it. Go," her friend and Legacy Witch replied.

"Dae, stay with Simone," she ordered the dog. "Watch her back while she concentrates on the door."

The vampire headed down the escalator steps. As she ran she said, "Maggie, the rear doors are booby trapped. I have to exit on the North end of the mall to reach the back."

"Okay, Annabeth . . . "

"Make sure the police know not to shoot me when I pop out."

"Sure, Annabeth . . . "

"I'm down to one pistol, a knife, and my sword. Any of those dhampirs snipers can take out will be helpful."

"They've been told. Annabeth . . ."

"What, Maggie? I'm trying to hurry."

"The police want to know if they are supposed to engage the indians?"

The sure-footed female stumbled rounding the escalator handrails on the first floor as she asked, "What indians?"

The braids of her red hair long since unraveled, she pushed through the single door at the end of the mall, bounded down a dozen steps, and turned toward the rear of the building. Rounding the corner, stepping into a service alley, she slammed to a stop as if hitting one of Simone's air-walls.

A phalanx of buckskin clad Native Americans with an assortment of weapons formed a semi-circle. Above them, ragged-clothed males and females worked down the building wall, using cracks, ledges, and drain pipes like experienced free climbers on a granite edifice. Well, perhaps drunken climbers as these creatures were none too graceful. They moved spastically, wracked by hunger and disoriented by the change leaving them somewhere between human and vampire. Annabeth knew their movements would change when they reached flat ground. They would have speed and strength greater than humans, without any of the controls of sanity. The hunger would drive them to locate prey.

The crack of a high-powered sniper rifle echoed between the mall and the structure on the other side of the ally. A body fell, landing a few feet from another lifeless corpse. Whether from the shots or the landing, their heads mutilated. She caught sight of the sniper using a single window high up on the rear building, and off to her far right. A great shot. In fact, two great shots considering the angles involved and the lack of consistency in the dhampirs' movements.

"Relax. We got this," a tiny voice told her.

She swung right, lifting the pistol with her left hand while holding the sword cross-wise in a defensive position. The little man flapped gossamer wings faster than a hummingbird to back up, hands out.

"Wait! I'm Justice. Fae. Dryad. Friend of the Dúnmharú," the wood nymph cried.

"Why are you here, and what is all of this?" Annabeth demanded.

"The Maerrighan called and told us about the trouble, and you being the Dúnmharú's betrothed, and him being sent to repay a favor, and we told Alohi, and he told Adahy, and they spoke with the others and the others said 'okay,' so we all came - the other dryads are Constance, Trust, Honor, Desireé, and Randi."

Five female nymphs flew to join them having heard their names. Each a different shade of green, but all ten-inches tall with wild dark auburn hair never introduced to a brush.

"The Native Americans are Nunnehi?" she asked.

"Of course," Justice answered, much more relaxed as the red-haired vampire holstered her pistol and lowered her sword.

"The Maerrighan asked you to help me as a favor?"

"Of course not," he replied, shocked at the question. "Asking for a favor is really dumb. She simply told us what was happening."

"The Nunnehi helped Arina try to destroy the unity of the three species by recruiting the Blood Dragons," she said. "Are they here to help me or help them?"

"Watch," the dryad said, pointing at the first dhampir to reach the alley.

A dozen shadow warriors converged on the unholy creature, surrounding it. They faded, the hybrid gone with them.

"They will take it to the forests and destroy it," Justice said. "A ceremony to cleanse its troubled soul will be performed before removing the head and burning the corpse."

As another partially turned vamp landed, the same thing occurred.

"We would have been here sooner but the cell phone's battery died and I lost gps. Do you know how hard it is to get directions from humans?" the small Fae asked as he hovered. The other five departed to watch the action from up close.

"Simone, you can stand down. All eight of the dhampirs are outside and being handled," she said, no longer bothering to transmit through Maggie with coms open to all.

"I still don't know why you or the Nunnehi are helping," Annabeth said. She sheathed her blade, sure the Shadow Warriors could handle the remaining dhampirs. She counted four on the wall, two bodies in the alley, and two already taken.

"First time I met the Dúnmharú he gave me tobacco," Justice said. "Really good tobacco. He smoked some with the Nunnehi leader, Adahy. Left a jar for them after giving me some for the dryads. A day ago a couple of humans showed up on the trail to Blood Mountain. They were putting a big crate in the woods next to the trail. More tobacco. I had to know, so I stopped them. After they got over meeting someone as special as myself, they told me Cahal Kearney commissioned them to deliver tobacco to this spot once a month. They had a special jar inside labeled For the Dryads. Tobacco from a land called Cornell'n'Diehl. Created by the Magician, Gregory Pease. And you know what we had to do for this treasure? Nothing. An act of friendship."

"The Fae do not interfere with battles between other races," a tall man in beaded buckskin and soft moccasin shoes said, materializing beneath the dryad. "I am Adahy of the Nunnehi. We are not like other Fae. We help our friends. We help our friends' friends."

"Your warriors are well trained and efficient," Annabeth said. She knew it was considered rude to say 'thank you' to a Fae. The compliment to Adahy's people would do the same thing, and be more appreciated.

"We trusted Arina, the one who led the vampires before you," he told her. "It may have been that misjudgment, or our own anger regarding humans which led us to find the mercenaries she needed to change the world. We will not trust again without more proof of integrity," he warned her.

The chief became a shadow, and then disappeared. The last of the dhampirs had landed and been taken. The alley now empty accept for a beautiful, well-armed, badly dressed vampire and six nude nymphs.

"Gotta go, nice to meet you, we'll give Maerrighan our new number when we find another cell phone, say hey to the Dúnmharú, bye." The six flew off, melting into the night sky.

"Annabeth?"

"Yes, Maggie."

"Everyone heard. Does this mean the Fae will be helping us settle things?"

"I have no idea," Annabeth admitted. "I know we lost some good people tonight for stupid reasons. I also know I have a team of unbelievably talented, courageous people."

"And a dog," Maggie responded.

"I included him in people," Annabeth replied. "He's one of us."

Chapter 24

"They are catching up," Epona said. She had the best view from Skerrit's back. "We will not reach the portal before they reach us."

The centaur came to a halt. He turned in a wide half-circle to face the pursuit. "Take the sword, Epona," he instructed the Fae. "If any of them get too close, make them pay for throwing you in that damn cell."

Cahal tossed Sionnach his sword. They did not have time to search for his weapons before escaping the black castle. The Dúnmharú was comfortable with his pair of Glochs and the combat knife he carried.

"Nice blade," Sionnach said, twirling it and finding the balance. "Vampire metal. Bishop?"

Cahal nodded. He did not know how the others dealt with being hybrids. He had talked with Skerrit about having a foot in two worlds, but the Fae Hunter and Centaur made it clear he did not change when his body did. He remained Skerrit regardless.

For Cahal, it was like having two distinct souls. A lighter human side tried to deal with things logically, avoiding conflict when it was not necessary. His darker soul, his Fae, acted more on instinct. When he allowed the darker part of him to control his actions, there was never a hesitation to act. Violence became another tool. He stood on the side of a roadway on a wild planet of inane and insane beings within a dimension of chaos. A good time to let the Fae take over.

Titania joined the pair, taking a spot between them.

"When Caileach finds out I am here, she will move the stars to get to me," she said.

"Damn it woman," the centaur snarled. "Do no use her name again. Especially not in this place. You'll be callin' the black bitch to you."

"They're on horseback," Epona said. "Perhaps I should try talking with their steeds."

"Only look like horses," Sionnach said. "These are demon-spawn with razor-sharp teeth, cloven hooves, and a taste for raw meat. Whatever rides them may be only half as dangerous. Keep that in mind. Do not let any of those animals near enough to bite or trample you."

"Skerrit, Titania, move further up the road," Cahal ordered. "Skerrit, prepare your bow. Anything able to get past us is yours. Titania, keep Skerrit between you and those riding in. Your presence could cause them to stop short and turn around."

"To tell the Queen," Titania finished his thought. "If they do not see me, they will press the attack."

"I need your helmet again," he told the Queen of the Seelie. Without hesitation she handed him her leather helm.

"Our best chance to escape is to silence them quickly," the Dúnmharú said. He turned to Sionnach and said, "Let them come to us. Stay your sword, and take this." He handed over Fin Bheara's cloak.

Sionnach wrapped the white cloth around his dirty clothing, hiding the sword beneath the folds.

"They may still recognize me," he said.

Cahal tossed the Queen's helmet to his father.

The blood-red helmet with face-guard looked like a demon-head floating above snow.

Skerrit cantered up the road, Epona on his back and Titania running within his shadow, her hand on his shoulder. When he turned, bow in hand, the Princess of Ponies disappeared behind his thick torso. Titania could not be seen, standing beside his rump on the shade-side of the sun.

Cahal moved away from Sionnach to take a position on the far side of the road. His hands down, near the pistols' butts.

"Impressive," Sionnach said. "The Queen of the Seelie, the second most powerful Fae Royal, the King of the Centaurs, and quite possibly the equal to Oberon in strength, and the King's personal bodyguard taking directions without comment. From a part-Fae, part-human who has lived less than three decades," he added.

"Should I have asked for a discussion?"

"No. You took command, and you did so without ego. We accepted your decisions because you expected nothing less. It is a rare gift you possess, Cahal. Anyone can take the lead, but few inspire others to accept their leadership without question."

"Bishop has been training me to become the Council of Four's Dúnmharú since I was twelve," the younger man said. "I'm expected to take charge and enforce rules. I'm also expected to protect the innocent. It's all part of the course."

"You did not learn how to take charge over some of the most powerful beings alive from schooling," Sionnach replied. He turned his head to watch the phooka and their riders descending upon them. "Your character determined your training. Bishop saw what you were and allowed you to release the Dúnmharú."

Cahal did not reply. They had more important things to deal with first.

Leanne pulled her beast back short of where the two men stood.

"Who are you?" she demanded.

"Who asks?" Cahal replied.

Taken aback, Leanne could not ever recall someone in Pandaemonium not recognizing her. The black in her eyes grew larger, pushing the white away. Her emotions waffled between anger and curiosity.

"Leanne Shee, daughter of the Black Queen, Dark Princess of Pandaemonium, Commander of the Vex, merciless warriors of the Neo-Fae Court, and the woman who will beat you to pulp and lick the blood from your corpse," she answered. "Now, who . . . are . . . you?"

Cahal dropped to a knee, Sionnach, surprised by the action, followed a breath later.

"Humble apologies Princess," Cahal said, chin buried in his chest. "I and my companion are mercenaries from a distant galaxy. We heard there might be a demand for our services in Pandaemonium."

Leanne stared at the light-brown hair covering the top of the kneeling man's head. She cast a look to the oddly dressed other, in white cloak and red helm. She returned her attention to the first one as her escort reined in their phooka behind her.

"You are going in the wrong direction, mercenary," she said.

"We visited the Black Castle, but the Queen was not in residence," he replied. "We decided to explore."

"A dangerous idea on this world," she answered. "Did you see the uber-trolls at the bridge?"

"Twice," Cahal responded. "Once coming in. They were in a heated argument so we passed quickly. On our way out we found them dead. It appeared they murdered each other."

"Maybe," she said. "And the centaur?"

"Another mercenary. When we saw you approach we separated, in case the trolls did not kill each other and the true murderer was trailing us."

Donagh worked his way through the five hybrid dark elves to sit his steed next to the Princess.

"It all sounds well enough," he said aloud. "But how did you enter Pandaemonium. The gate is warded by the Queen's magik."

While Princess Leanne engaged the handsome mercenary, keeping the attention of her guard on their give-and-take, Sionnach rose slowly and made his way a little forward. Only Leanne's phooka seemed to notice, keeping a distrustful eye on the strange creature with the red head.

When the others realized the stranger's story fell apart, and hands went to hilts, Sionnach opened the cape. He slashed the Cerrul sword across the withers of a phooka carrying a slender male elf the color of wood smoke. The animal reared in pain, dropped and nearly fell when its weight could not be borne on the injured front quarter.

The elf tumbled over the bloody shoulder, landing hard on his back upon the firm roadway. Sionnach slashed down.

The dark elves were the result of centuries of mixing and matching bloodlines by the Black Queen, magicians, and alien scientists hired or coerced into assisting her vision of creating an UnSeelie race of Neo-Fae. She assigned them to protect the one being in the seven dimensions who sparked the tiniest flame of care within the solemn sovereign.

Caelan, the grey-skinned thin elf, surprised and thrown, displayed the reflexes of his breeding. He blocked Sionnach's blade with a knife wrenched from a boot sheath in a blink of an eye.

The knife, forged in a volcano's fire from iron found in a meteor, was incredibly hard. It shattered beneath the blue metal from the world of vampires. It did, however, deflect Sionnach aim. Instead of driving into and across the elf's chest, the tip slipped through his leather jerkin and pierced his shoulder.

The injured phooka twisted and twirled on three legs, slamming into the other animals, forcing riders to concentrate on holding their seats.

Leanne's head went from the action behind her, to snapping around when she realized they were under attack. Her overconfidence allowed them to bunch together as she felt two men on foot would be no trouble for the seven most skilled warriors in the Neo-Fae army.

She knew about firearms, had seen some, but the Queen, a full-blooded original Fae, would not tolerate them. The young man in the black outfit held two.

Donagh, his instinct to protect the Princess bred and beaten into him, urged his steed forward at the first movement by Sionnach. Six steel-jacketed 9-mm bullets peppered his stomach and chest. One entered below his chin and exited through shattered teeth. If he had not acted automatically, they would have hit Leanne.

The shots burned like hellfire, and the nerves in his face screamed. He ignored the pain, sliding off the phooka with his double-handed curved single-edged sword out and up by the time his feet hit the ground. Blood gushed from his injured mouth and dribbled out of the slug's entry hole onto his chest. His focus completely on the brown-haired, brown-eyed assassin who attempted to kill his duty.

Keara, the buxom black female, leaped from her seat to stand over the fallen Caelan, forcing Sionnach to step back as she crisscrossed two matching wide blades similar to butterfly swords once used by the ancient Chinese on Earth.

"Cornus, Nola, Odhran," Leanne yelled. "Go kill the centaur. We should be finished by the time you return."

The three dark elves did not hesitate, launching their phooka forward with sharp spurs. They did manage to draw and swing blades at Cahal as they rushed between him and the guard captain.

The Princess of Pandaemonium threw a long leg over her animal's neck. She slipped off to the side, the blue metal of her own sword catching the sun's rays, flashing yellow and red along the razor edge. She took her place beside Donagh. His blood, infused with adrenaline and sweat, enraged her thirst. After the stranger was done with, she would end his suffering by taking every drop left within his body.

She lost the blood lust quickly when the man who claimed to be a mercenary calmly fired two bullets into her right knee. Her leg exposed by the filmy dress, and her boots not high enough to cover her knees.

The leg gave way. She landed on the injured knee, eliciting a scream of pain laced with anger. The pain cleared her head. For the first time she actually looked at the man who crippled her.

Before, riding up on the pair, she immediately noticed the man in black, waiting calmly before her charge. As she neared she found his stature pleasing, and his face pleasant. Her thoughts went to images of discovering how he would look naked in her bed. Her fangs nipping, and her tongue tasting his rich blood. And sex. As they talked, him on bended knee, she felt the dual lust for blood and cock.

Now she truly saw him, and it frightened her. He maintained the same calm demeanor within a whirl of deadly activity. His eyes flat, his face devoid of hate, excitement, fear, or pleasure. She felt fear because his cold-hearted bearing was exactly like her mother's. Not cruel. Not happy. Do what must be done, get it over, move on.

He easily danced away from the trio of phooka. With minimal movement, he avoided her elves' blades. Without concern he shot her and turned his attention to Donagh. She wanted badly to fuck his brains out right now, on the dirty roadway, in the midst of blood and death.

The Guard Captain's moved without the natural flow he used his entire life. The injuries and the loss of blood made him slower. He felt he jerked instead of walked. Watching Princess Leanne dropped by the bastard's guns, hearing her screams, reinvigorated him.

"You will die," he yelled, leaping at the stranger, his trusted tanto style sword plunging down with the might of a genetically enriched soldier.

With his teeth badly damaged and blood welling in his mouth, the shout came out "Udullí!"

The Dúnmharú waited for the elf to fully commit to the forward slash before sliding to his right. The move allowed the blade to slash through air. Donagh's strength and anger buried the sharp forward curve into the ground. Cahal placed a Gloch against the elf's left wrist and fired, holding the trigger until the clip emptied.

Donagh's wrist disintegrated. He fell back with a bloody stump gushing more of his life-blood. His useless hand released its grip on the hilt and fell.

Leanne, her Fae-Vampire metabolism shaking off the wounds to her knee, the structure already in the middle-stages of revivification, stood. She kept her weight on her good left leg. With his firearm empty, she would take his head. The sword vibrated in her hand, ready for the kill.

Chapter 25

"Three of 'em coming," Skerrit told Epona and Titania. "Silly."

He fired a steel-tipped arrow at the elf in the lead. The first UnSeelie looked different from the others. A horn protruded from his forehead. The abnormality the result of the Black Queen's experimental use of dark elf genes, unicorn DNA, and magik.

The fair-skinned elf with flowing Palomino-colored locks cut the arrow with his sword.

"Talented," the centaur said. "He took the arrow while at a full gallop. This may be interesting after all."

"Don't get cocky, Skerrit," Titania said, still standing in the shadow thrown by the huge body of a horse. "They will be more than they appear."

"Hmmmmm," the Hunter replied, firing two arrows, one following the other in less than a breath.

Cornus took the first shaft out of the air as he did earlier, and twisted to the side to avoid the second. Nola, the stark white female in his wake realized she was in its path with only enough time to duck. The sharp point grazed her skull. Blood tinted her snow-white hair pink.

Skerrit adjusted his aim and fired again. Cornus thought the archer was losing his nerve until the arrow pierced his thigh. He reached down to pull the shaft out, stopping when he realized the tip included hinged barbs. Once though, they opened. Any attempt to pull it would result in more damage. His hand ached from the touch of cold iron. The shaft was metal.

As he slowed, Nola, then Odhran, the short, pale green member of the elite guard, passed. Neither thought to assist. Their duty lay in slaying the centaur.

The white elf lifted her feet and crouched atop the phooka. Letting the chains go, hands now filled with eight-inch daggers, she used her strength to launch herself over the head of the charging animal, directly at the torso of the centaur's human-portion.

Skerrit smiled at the flying elf. His eyes held respect for her ability and bravery. They also spoke to her foolishness.

She screamed a battle cry. He ducked.

Nola sailed over the lowered head and body straight into Skerrit's sword. Epona held the mighty cutter in both hands, braced by her thighs tightly pressed against the stallion's body. The tip entered the elf's open mouth and exited with an explosive effect, sending shards of skull and a spray of grey matter into the air.

After decades of captivity and deprivation, the Fae Royal retained the strength to hold the skewered elf aloft.

"Could you get that thing off my back?" Skerrit asked. "It's drippin' blood and goo all over me."

Epona lowered the dead elf, allowing gravity to slide the head the length of the sword.

Odhran, chasing behind the white dark elf, planned to take advantage of the centaur's lowered head and torso. His ducking Nola exposed the nape of his neck. The green elf's long blade would easily separate head from shoulders.

He held the sword in the backhand style of a cavalry charge, allowing the force created by the speed of his steed to deliver the killing blow.

His arm nearly wrenched from his socket when Titania stepped forward and blocked his sword with her own.

The sound of metal on metal rang across the landscape.

Odhran continued past. He yanked the chains and used the painful bit to pivot his phooka. Before him Nola lay dead. A woman in red leathers stood with feet apart and short sword resting in her right hand. On the back of the centaur sat the red-headed Seelie captive held in the Black Castle. The Fae, no longer captive, held a sword much too large for her. The centaur began pulling arrows from a quiver at astounding speed. Notching, pulling, and releasing so quickly his arm and hand appeared to be more than one appendage. Too many missiles for the wounded Cornus to dodge or block. As Odhran watched, feathers appeared across the horned-elf's torso and legs. So many hits he looked like a strange bird.

Cornus fell. With so many arrows piercing his body, he seemed to float above the ground, held up by exposed tips and barbed heads. Lifeless eyes peered into the bright sun.

"The green one is coming back," Epona said.

"I'm finished with the unicorn," Skerrit responded. "Titania, do you need help?"

"I think not," the Fae Queen replied. The daughter of Titans. Relative to beings who held worlds upon their shoulders and pushed islands together to create continents.

The elf drove the phooka directly at her. The animal's eyes blazed. Blood, snot, and mucus foaming and spraying from its mouth, savaged by the metal bit. Whipped by chains, spurred with silver, it ran to release its pain and fury on the woman taunting in her red.

Titania's raised right palm connected with the phooka's chest. The beast ceased moving. Had it run full steam into a solid wall of granite, it would not have stopped any quicker than running into her open hand.

The short green elf flew over the head of the animal, arms spread, eyes wide, unable to believe what occurred.

The wild beast collapsed, dead from its heart stopping.

"Shame," the Queen murmured. She turned and walked in the direction of the flying elf.

He hit ungracefully, rolled and tumbled; twisted and turned. He came to a halt beside the dead Captain of the Guard. Rising to his full five-feet, he faced the beautiful woman in red. He noted her auburn hair, braided for battle, and the brilliant blue color of her eyes.

The elf, through all of his bodily gyrations, held firm his long sword. The others made fun of the shortest member of the guard having the longest blade. He joked it matched his cock in length and danger. It was more than twice the length of the woman's weapon.

When she reached a point too far for her to hit him, but close enough for his blade to kill, he swung with all his might, spinning to add velocity to the blow.

The blade made no contact, and the lack of resistance kept him spinning until he could catch his balance. He faced toward Air. The centaur and the captive stood before him.

"I'm not only strong," a sweet voice said in his ear, "I'm fast."

Titania, having moved aside and forward to avoid the spiraling assault, stood behind the little green man. She took his head.

Lunging forward to land on her strong left leg, Leanne thrust her sword into the stranger's torso, faster than any snake on Pandaemonium could strike.

The tip landed, penetrated beyond the black cloth of Cahal's shirt and grazed his abs. His Fae-enhanced skin resisted most edged weapons. Projectiles, like bullets and arrows, bruised him, but did not cause wounds. Cerrulan metals, billeted and forged into blades, cut him as they would anyone.

"Quick," he said in appreciation of Leanne Shee's attack. Then he shot her in the left knee with the second pistol.

She went down again. This time without a whimper. She grounded her sword to accept her weight and prevent her total collapse. Coal black eyes, behind hair stringy and flat from sweat, fired cliche beams of hate at the insufferable male.

Cahal kept an eye on the Princess, aware of her ability to heal, and her desire to slaughter him. He calmly dropped the spent clips from the two Glochs and inserted fresh ones. He emptied one into the dying elf. Blood loss and shock would soon take the being, regardless of its genetics. The twelve rounds ended his suffering.

As he replaced the spent clip with another from his belt, he watched his father. Sionnach fenced with the black elf long enough for the skinny one to recover from the shoulder wound.

"Are you playing with them for a reason?" he called to the original half-human, half-Fae.

"An opportunity to test an opponent should never be wasted," the Fae warrior called back. "These dark elves were chosen to guard the Princess. You would hope the reason is their ability to guard the Princess."

The female with the butterfly swords continued to press her attack. She was fast, displayed stamina, as the duel with Sionnach lasted several minutes, and limber. She changed levels easily. Her legs lashed out as often as her blades.

Caelan held back. He shivered in anger and consternation. His own blade laid shattered and useless. He could engage without a weapon, but he would be more of a distraction to Keara than an opponent to the bastard who broke his knife.

A sharp whistle caused him to whip his head toward the first stranger. Donagh lay dead. No big loss. The Princess knelt in agony, her weight hanging on her sword. A tragedy. The stranger held Donagh's long sword. Incredibly, he tossed the weapon to the elf.

Armed, he went to Keara's left side. Though she used double swords, she favored her right hand. He would protect and attack from her left.

"Really?" Sionnach asked. Cahal shrugged.

"An opportunity to learn from an ally should never be wasted," Cahal answered.

"When you allow your Fae rein, you are quite the bastard," Titania said, joining him to watch Sionnach defend against two elves.

"I keep telling the lad he needs to do it more often," Skerrit said, standing behind them, Epona on his back.

Not interested in providing a show, and more concerned about wasting time that could result in more UnSeelie arrivals, Sionnach demonstrated why Oberon named his son his personal bodyguard.

He thrust the Cerrulan blade into Keara's chest as she completed a double crossing move with her swords. As her hands parted, the sword's tip slipped through and entered between her breasts. SIonnach pushed, driving the blade deeper. Then he turned the elf, using the sword as a lever.

Caelan swung the two-handed sword from over his head, pushing with his top hand and pulling with his bottom hand. A classic slashing technique which added power while maintaining precision. He intended to cut across the interloper's arms, but caught Keara's shoulder instead. Sionnach's had twisted the mortally wounded woman into Caelan's path.

Horrified, the slender elf froze long enough for the half-Fae to recover his sword. He lunged. The return thrust passed underneath Keara's armpit and into Caelan's throat.

The black elf's dying body finally gave way as the blue steel came away from her companion's neck, once more traveling beneath her arm. She began to crumple.

Sionnach swung the sword over his head and came back crosswise, turning his hips into the delivery. The scalpel-sharp edge took the thin elf's head. It did not perceptibly slow through its downward angle, maintaining the force needed to decapitate the black dark elf's as she fell.

"Two heads with a single swing," Skerrit said. "Could notta done better myself."

Sionnach wiped the blade across Keara's tunic, aware of Leanne's hate-filled gaze. As he walked across the blood-splattered roadway to join the others, he used Cahal's sword to knock Leanne's up, hitting it a second time to loft it, catching it by the hilt in his left hand.

Without the added support, the UnSeelie Royal fell to her hands. Once more she grimaced as her battered knees took the brunt. Once more refusing to give voice to her pain or frustration.

"When have you ever taken two heads with one swing?" Sionnach asked the centaur.

"That hydra in Crete," the Hunter answered. "Damn thing had nine noggins, and two got tangled together. Couldn't take one without the other."

"Four grew back," Titania reminded him.

"True dat," he replied with a low laugh. "But I had my fun, so I let the beast live."

"Big of you," Sionnach said.

He removed the leather helmet and handed it to Titania with a nod of thanks. He returned Cahal's sword to him.

"I'll keep this one," indicating the one taken from the Princess. "She won't be needing it in hell."

"Keep the sword, but we're not killing her," Cahal said, bringing scowls and furrowed brows from all, including Leanne.

"I'm worthless as a hostage," the young Neo-Fae said. "The Queen will go through me to get to you. It will not bother her in the least."

A giant dragon with orange-red scales, matching eyes, and flames slipping from its nostrils as well as the sides of a mouth filled with jagged fangs, rose from the gully.

"You better run like never before," the dark princess screamed. "My dragon will turn you all to ash!"

Epona said, "A pretty fair illusion. Needs some work on the shadowing."

"Work of a child," Skerrit said. "I can scant see the damn thing. No smell of brimstone, no reek of rotten breath. Worthless."

"Her mother is known as the Queen of Air and Darkness because of her ability to create incredible glamours out of the air. The daughter seems to have inherited a smidgen of the talent," Titania said.

Sionnach said nothing, leaning on the stolen sword as if using a golf club while awaiting his turn to play.

Cahal holstered his pistols and placed his sword within its sheath. He went to the phooka slashed by Sionnach early in the confrontation. The animal was on its side, dying. He used his knife to cut the chains. He gently removed the hated bit, tossing it far away. He placed a gentle hand over the one eye on his side, pulled his pistol, placed it at the base of the beast's skull and ended its pain.

"Thank you, Cahal," Epona whispered.

The Dark Princess watched without comment. The illusionary dragon faded. She kept her eyes on the strange stranger as he came toward her.

Pistol holstered, he put his foot between Leanne's shoulders and pushed her flat onto the ground. He used the chains to tie her hands, pulling them up and back, creating a painful looking arch. He finished by wrapping the end of the chains around her ankle, careful of the spurs. He secured her arms and legs forcing the woman into a bow. If she tried to lower her shoulders or legs, the chains tightened, biting into her skin.

"Kill me now," she spoke the words calmly. She channeled all of her pain, anger, frustration, and despair into the semblance of cold she saw in her mother, and now in this stranger. "If not, I swear my revenge will be terrible."

Cahal ignored her.

"We need to pick up the pace," he told the others. He sped off in the direction of the exit gate.

Chapter 26

Arina's study was large, well appointed, and came with floor to ceiling windows which framed a manicured lawn, large swimming pool, and the cloud reflected lights of Atlanta. The city surrounded them on all sides. The barrier walls with security systems allowed the lights to be seen, while keeping anything else out.

Annabeth sat in a comfortable executive chair. Comfortably tilted back, her boot-shod feet crossed at the ankle, planted on the top of Arina's prized antique desk.

Dae snoozed on a lounge in front of a window. He claimed the spot the moment they entered the room. A hose in the garage used to wash blood and gunk from his hair before he was allowed indoors.

The others plopped onto any soft surfaces.

Simone Sinclair, Maggie Giamonte, Michele Quan, Rusty Toole, Camila Raoul, Harry Campbell, Grant Franco, Cindy Sommers, and Kristy Nichol all present.

Everyone would be required to provide full reports for the FBI and the Atlanta Police, but no one detained them. They could not take the bodies of Tom Farway or James McWaters until after the forensics teams completed their work. They would be transported to the morgue. The coroner would call in a day or two to arrange for the Council to have them flown back to the UK.

Ché was locked away in the basement. No one in authority objected to the new Overlord providing the secure cell necessary to hold a two-thousand-year-old vampire. The Atlanta P.D. held the two surviving human servants. They needed the optics of an arrest for the news reports. Annabeth received assurances she would be able to interview them upon request, even if it meant the middle of the night.

"The sun will be up in another hour," Annabeth said. "First, I cannot begin to tell you how proud I am of all of you. Second, if anyone wishes to remain on my new team, you are more than welcome."

"You can call me whenever," Simone said. "I've always been on Team Annabeth. But I have my own responsibilities. When you rise I will be home in Quebec. Most likely in my bed recovering from exhaustion."

"I'll hug you later," the redhead said. "I'm too comfortable to move right now."

"It was an experience," Harry Campbell said. "I did my time in the military, but I prefer my gig flying those sweet Gulfstreams for the Council. I'll ask if I can stay to take Tom and James back, but I won't be coming back."

"Understood, and appreciated," Annabeth replied. "If I could fly away from this I would. Anyone else?"

"I'll miss the jets, but I have never felt this jazzed in my life," Kristy chimed. "I can't wait to see what crap you have to deal with next."

"Thanks, I think," the response. "We may fix that jet-addiction of yours. I'm going to have a lot of trips to make, and I'll need a fast plane and a good pilot."

"Hired," Kristy answered, fist pump to the ceiling.

"I'd like to stay," Raoul said, her eyes cut toward the brunette pilot.

"Me, too," Toole said. "Hated the rent-a-cop deal. Much prefer the vampire Overlord's mercenary hitman title."

"Great," Annabeth said. "I get a talented former US Ranger and a new rent-a-hit guy."

Everyone chuckled or snorted at Toole's expense.

"I didn't get to do much, but I'd like to stay, too," Cindy Sommers said.

"Same," Grant Franco added. "But not if I'm going to be left on bouncer duty watching a door."

"You both proved you could follow orders and handle yourselves under stress," Annabeth responded, giving the compliments easily. She knew the value of a well-placed vocal reward. "I'll make sure you both get cannon-fodder placements the next time we go up against unbeatable numbers."

Dae moaned and muffled mini-growls and harrumphs while his four feet twitched.

"He's either chasing squirrels or he just signed on to the team," Simone joked. For a woman known world-wide as the Ice Witch, she showed a lot of warmth among her new colleagues.

"At least until Cale returns," Annabeth said. She could not disguise the sadness in her tone.

"He's coming back," Kristy said. "I'm determined to put him on a plane and actually land with him still aboard."

"That's the problem when you ask for a favor," Simone said. "There's always the payback. Remember that, Annabeth Hughes, Overlord of the Southeastern Territory, and newest member to the Vampire Directorate. Bishop and Ssara Den both owe you for asking this favor from you. I'd say you earned whatever you demand in return."

"Here, Here!" Rusty Toole called, raising a pretend glass. "To Annabeth Hughes, Overlord!"

The others raised imaginary glasses and repeated, "To Annabeth Hughes, Overlord!"

She raised her hand in salute without lifting her feet from the desk. "To me," she whispered. "And fucking favors."

Daegen snorted in his sleep.

Chapter 27

"Now what?" Skerrit asked.

Epona peeked around his shoulder. She released a shriek in his ear, and leapt from the top of the centaur to the ground with the ease of a gymnast and the excitement of a child on its birthday.

A pack of Yeth Hounds, likely the same ones they encountered on their journey to Darkness, gathered on the roadway.

The shriek startled Skerrit, and the Fae female was off and running before he could act. He notched an arrow and prepared to take the first canine to act aggressively.

Cahal, Sionnach, and Titania hurried forward, having taken to walking behind the centaur to watch for anyone attempting to overtake.

"That fool woman," Sionnach said, raising his new-found weapon.

Cahal placed a hand on his father's shoulder, preventing him from rushing to Epona's aid.

"Wait," he said. An easy confidence in the single word.

"I hope you're right," Titania said.

Epona launched herself into the middle of a pack of monstrous animals with heads like hounds and bodies like oversized Swiss Mountain Dogs.

Skerrit broke the tension as he began to laugh. The pack of beasts became a tangle of litter puppies, Epona included. As large and ferocious as they were, the Yeth Hounds nuzzled and rubbed against the slender Fae carefully. Excited and mindful she was less than healthy.

The four hybrid warriors continued forward to join the party. Epona sat on the ground, surrounded by her friends.

"We must take them with us," she said. "They do not belong in Pandaemonium. I will never leave them."

"No worries," Cahal said, once more speaking as the team's leader without considering a discussion with the other, older, more powerful beings with him. "We need to go. The sun is dropping quickly, and I believe darkness will be in the favor of the Queen of Air and Darkness."

The strange group on a stranger world raced toward the horizon and beckoning foothills. A Fae riding the wide back of a centaur, surrounded by a pack of running Yeth Hounds followed by a Queen, a warrior, and the Dúnmharú.

The young woman arrived at the head of a cavalry. She ordered the one-hundred mounted Neo-Fae to a halt as they rode upon the site of Leanne Shee on her stomach, tied like an animal prepared for a spit. Two dead phooka and the bodies of elves littered the roadway.

She removed her grey helmet and shook loose long, straight white hair. A midnight blue streak ran from her crown to the tips of her hair in the middle of her right tresses.

Tossing a long leg over her steed's neck, she slid gracefully to the ground. Leather knee boots of dove grey below darker grey jodhpurs. The medium-length sword with intricate hand guard slapped lightly against her thigh as she walked to stand before the helpless Dark Princess.

The woman eased into a cross-legged sit before Leanne. Her dark grey blouse of fine linen loosely tied by a cord of matching color, left untied at the top. Silky porcelain breasts swelled beneath the soft material, cleavage exposed behind the lacing.

"Are you going to sit and gloat, Sister, or are you going to get me out of these chains?" Leanne asked.

"I need to take this in, Sister. It will be a memory to hold and cherish. I may wish to entertain my children with it one day," the woman answered.

Having discovered the power incarnate with setting emotions aside, Leanne did not berate her younger sibling, or scream at her.

"Take your time, Leathe. The ones who did this are only getting closer to the exit portal while you relish my humiliation. Mother will be angry with me for my failure. She may as well add you for allowing the two Fae she held in the dungeons to escape."

Leathe Dimoni, the Grey Princess of Pandaemonium, daughter of the Black Queen and the King of the Kingdom of Shadows in the fifth dimension rose from her seat as easily as she settled.

The grey-alloy rapier, thin and deadly, made from metals found only in the fifth dimension, sliced through the chains with ease.

"You can ride behind my Captain," she told her older sister.

Leanne, the time spent tied enough for her wounded knees to mend, walked with the posture befit a royal to the forward line of the cavalry. She passed the tall Captain seated upon his karkadann. The animal a mix of unicorn and something like a rhinoceros. The unicorn horn lower, set below the animal's eyes instead of its forehead. Thick grey skin like armor and the legs of a thoroughbred. No mane, and a whip-thin tail a meter long.

Leanne grabbed the leg of the rider next to the Captain and pulled him forcefully from his steed. In one fluid motion she was seated. Then she was gone, racing across the roadway toward Air.

Leathe, laughing, collected a crumpled white cloak from the dusty roadway, donned her helmet, mounted her karkadann and followed with the cavalry. The hapless UnSeelie Leanne dismounted trampled beneath their surge.

"From the size of the dust cloud, I would estimate an entire army is on its way," Skerrit said. He transformed to humanoid when they arrived at the portal.

Eyes turned to the road below the hill and back toward the Black Castle.

"Titania, you and Skerrit go through first when I clear the ward," Cahal said. "You need to make sure Morgan does not attack when the Yeth Hounds come through."

"We're not plane-traveling directly back to the grassland world," Skerrit reminded him.

"And you think Morgan will not be at the in-between?" the part-Fae asked.

"Of course she will be," Skerrit agreed. "She'll have left Fin Bheara to set up defenses while she waited to cover our asses if something followed us out of Pandaemonium."

"Bheara's cape," Sionnach grumbled. "I left the damn thing behind. One more reason for him to hate my soul. Who is Morgan?"

"Morrigan," Skerrit said. "Your lad could no say her name properly when he was wee. It stuck."

"She allowed it?" the half-Fae warrior asked, obviously wondering how much had changed on Earth in the short time he and Oberon were gone.

"I think she likes it," Titania said. "But only when Cahal or Annabeth use it."

"Annabeth?"

"We have to go," Cahal said, interrupting any more information or questions.

"Epona, you follow Skerrit and have the hounds follow you. Sionnach and I will come last. I'll reset the ward."

He placed his left hand against the unseen magical wall and said the incantation-mantra aloud. The barrier shimmered, but did not fall.

"I can see a rider out front," Skerrit said. "I'm pretty sure it's your new girlfriend."

"Sionnach. Help." Cahal called for the assistance while adding as much personal will to the magic held in check by the ring on his left hand.

His sire placed his left hand and similar ring against the force of the ward. While Cahal spoke his words, Sionnach spoke the same words backwards, which was forward, which is confusing. But it worked.

The barrier seemed to glow and then turned to embers and dissipated.

Titania rushed through, followed by the two-legged centaur. Epona spoke urgently to her pack, turned and followed Skerrit. As soon as she disappeared into the waiting tunnel, the hounds hurried to the gateway and stopped. They scented and shied from the portal.

"Go!" Cahal ordered the animals. The power of all things within him congealed within the one simple word. The pack went through, yelping like hounds on a fox hunt.

Cahal and Sionnach stepped into the tunnel, turned, raised their hands and repeated their mantras. This time Sionnach spoke the words in reverse while Cahal said them in the ancient Latin tongue. Thirteen Of Twelve.

When Leathe caught Leanne, the Dark Princess sat serenely atop her appropriated mount, eyes on the exit portal cave entrance set on the hillside above.

"Only Mother can release the barrier wards on the gates," Leathe said.

"Apparently not," Leanne replied.

"Any idea who they were?"

"Having listened to Mother's reasons for hating all things Seelie since we were too small to walk, I know exactly who they are," the Dark Princess said.

The Grey Princess waited. Finally she asked, "Well?"

"You know Epona, the captured Fae Royal who talks to animals."

"Used to go down in the dungeons and watch her draw in the dirt. Not particularly entertaining," Leathe replied.

"The other one we captured after Oberon escaped is known as Sionnach Catharnagh. The Warrior Fox, hybrid assassin and personal guard for Oberon. He used his own magic to open the ward and allow his king to flee while he fought our army."

"Yeah, yeah. I was there. He killed a hundred Neo-Fae and mercenaries before we could throw a net on him. Mother reinforced the wards so he couldn't bring them down again. Handsome bastard. I wanted to chain him and ride his big cock, but Mother wouldn't allow it. I think she had her own plans. Maybe another sibling for us," she said. The smirk was not reflected as humor in her dead-grey eyes. No emotion ever showed in Leathe's grey eyes. The windows to her soul forever shaded.

"The centaur was Skerrit, the Fae Hunter, Leader of the Wild Rides, and last Ipotane."

"Makes sense. He would be the most likely one sent back by Oberon."

"The woman in red leathers was Queen Titania."

Leathe's mouth dropped open.

"Titania? You sure? You let the one person our Mother hates the most escape? Queen Titania was in Pandaemonium. She was actually here. Mother never knew. She didn't feel the presence of the woman who stole her birthright. You sure it was Titania?"

"I'm sure," Leanne answered.

"You are so screwed."

The Dark Princess remained emotionless. If the Black Queen would punish her for Titania entering their world, rescuing the captives, and escaping then she would. Fearing it would not prevent it. Worrying about what the punishment would be could not make it easier.

"There was one more," her sister said.

"That one I do not know," Leanne replied. "Epona whispered his name, Cahal. It means dark."

"Dark? Like you are the Dark Princess?"

"I intend to find out," Leanne said. No. Swore. "I will find Cahal and I will teach him what true darkness means."

"If Mother ever lets you out of the dungeons," Leathe responded, pivoting the karkadann. She pushed through the UnSeelie hoard and raced for Darkness.

Leanne sat her ride quiescent for a few minutes. Eyes on the gate, her mind elsewhere. Then she followed Leathe back to Darkness. Fate awaited. She needed to ask her mother a favor.

Chapter 28

The party was epic. Directly non-proportional to the uneventful plane-travels from Pandaemonium to the way-planet (where the Maerrighan waited), to the grasslands (where Titania informed Bheara he needed to purchase a new cloak), and through a myriad of exits and entrances until they arrived at Tir na Nog.

Oberon met them. The Yeth Hounds were allowed to run free. Epona promised they would not hunt, but would return to be fed at the King's castle in the world of Faery after exploring their new home.

They crossed the passage from Tir na Nog to Earth. The King's Castle there included several modern conveniences, things like multi-head hot showers. Titania took Epona and introduced her to the joys of human plumbing.

Back in his room, Cahal soon stood beneath a half-dozen sprays. He let the sweat, blood, and stink of Pandaemonium wash down the drain.

"Did you need to say something to me?" he asked.

Morgan stood at the shower doorway. The curtain pulled back. She wore a dress of raven-feathers.

"Your favor is repaid in full," she said. "Sionnach is in our chambers preparing for the King's welcome home party. Epona is being fitted for new clothes. She looks wonderful. Having her back will lift the hearts of many Fae. Titania is quite pleased with you. Skerrit is telling stories that will be retold for centuries. You come off as something of a hero."

"Sionnach tell you anything of interest?"

"Some. He is bothered you would not allow him to kill the Black Queen's daughter. He does not know you, Cahal. He does, however, know the oracle of the Dúnmharú. The Enforcer. The Assassin. He wonders if you are the one prophesied."

"Someone will have to tell me that prophesy," he said. He let the hot water stream over his shoulders, allowing pent up tension a release. "Murderer. The first time I looked up Dúnmharú, the first translation was murderer. Perhaps the best description, but I could not murder Leanne Shee."

"Why?"

"Because she is your niece, Morgan," he said. "Because I saw some of you in her. Maybe not enough to ever make her less Un-Seelie, but enough I could not take the chance from her."

"You are so very young, Cahal," the Fae Royal feared by every Fae replied. She also smiled. A rare event in this or any dimension. "I have a present for you."

"Please, not Shaylee again," he said to her back. "I can't. I don't have the stamina."

Morgan stepped away. Annabeth Hughes stood there. Beautiful, naked Annabeth. She stepped into the sprays and molded her cool skin against his. Her mouth found his; her hand wrapped around his growing penis.

She leaned back, her nipples hard atop firm breasts, and her emerald green eyes alive.

"Who is Shaylee?"

"I thought I was going to die," Annabeth said.

She leaned against Cale in a corner of the huge banquet hall. She wore a green silk dress designed to accent her curves and expose her gorgeous legs. It was the exact color of her eyes. Titania's own dressmaker delivered the creation to Cahal's room.

He wore a cream-colored shirt tucked into black linen slacks. They made a perfect match. Only the entrance of Oberon and Titania received more raucous applause than when they arrived to the party.

"Puked my guts out every time Morgan transported me," Cale said in empathy.

"Have you spent much time with Sionnach?"

"No. It's been too hectic. Besides, we both are weirded-out over the father-son thing. May take some time before we are comfortable together."

"My, what a mature attitude," the redhead vampire said. "What did Pandaemonium do to my boyfriend?"

"What did Bishop do to my girlfriend? Overlord of the Southeast Territory of North America. Member of the Vampire Directorate. Hero of Atlanta. Oberon's Castle has television. You are something of a superstar."

"Responsibilities," she muttered. "Yuck. But the perks are cool. I have a team."

"Not a coterie?"

"Not yet," she answered. "It's going to take some time and effort to get Arina's controls broken completely. I expect help from the Dúnmharú. Speaking of help. Nunnehi and dryads? Tobacco? What is up with that?"

"I'll tell you all about it when we get to the island house," he answered. "Before I can join your team, you need to help me rebuild my home. And return my dog."

"I can handle nightshift repairs," she joked, "but I may have to keep the mutt. I kinda like him."

"We can discuss sharing," he answered, pulling her into a kiss.

"Excuse me."

"Bishop," Cale responded to the interruption. "They invited everyone to this party."

"I came after I heard what happened in Pandaemonium," he said. "I've asked Oberon for a private meeting. You need to be there."

The invitation did not specifically include Annabeth, but it did not exclude her either.

They followed the Exemplar non-terrestrial vampire through a side door, down a short hall, and into a cozy chamber.

Since his earliest days in the King's Castle, it amazed Cale how many rooms with stone walls, stone floors, and stone ceilings could be made warm and welcoming with rugs, tapestries, lighting, and comfortable furniture.

Oberon, Titania, Skerrit, Morgan, and Epona waited inside. No one sat.

"What holds such importance, Bishop?" the King asked.

"We need to wait for Sionnach," the vampire replied. "I asked him to bring something."

They waited. The silence a stark contrast to the gaiety of the King's homecoming party, combined into a celebration of Sionnach's rescue and Epona's return.

Sionnach entered with the sword he appropriated from the Dark Princess.

"Here it is," he said, handing the naked blade to Bishop. "I haven't had time to find a sheath."

Bishop took the sword, examining the filigree, the guard, the hilt, handle wrapping, and shape of the blade.

"It's Cerrulan," he said.

"We know," Sionnach said.

"It's a Cerrulan blade cast for a specific person. In this case, the runes etched below the hilt name the blade's owner. From Cerrul to old latin, it is basically Tenebris Domina Heredis."

"Dark Lady Heir," Cale translated aloud.

"Dark Princess," Bishop replied.

"We know it is Leanne Shee's sword," Sionnach said. His tone bored.

"Epona, did you learn anything of the Black Queen's family while imprisoned?" Bishop asked.

"Between the visitors, the guards, and the Queen's children coming to gawk and make fun of me, I heard some things," she replied.

"Leanne Shee's sire?"

"The Black Queen took a vampire from the Cerrul dimension. I had the impression he was not exactly from Cerrul, but connected."

"Vampires are sterile," Annabeth said. "A vampire could not father the Dark Princess."

"Magik can accomplish many things," Oberon said. "Perhaps because this vampire was related to those of Cerrul, but not exactly Cerrulan himself allowed Caileach to become pregnant."

Skerrit nearly jumped out of his skin at the Queen's real name, but stopped himself from berating the King.

"Perhaps," Bishop murmured. "Regardless, the blade was made from metals found only on Cerrul." He swung the weapon easily. "Forged by a Cerrulan swordsmith. He bound the sword to the owner."

"It was Leanne Shee's, and now it is mine," Sionnach said. "Is there a point?"

Bishop brought the sword to rest. Edge up, the spine resting in his free hand.

"When a sword and a soul are bound, the ancient magic keeps the two connected until the person dies," he told his audience. "This remains Leanne Shee's weapon. More importantly, she can follow it. Anywhere. Even across the dimensional gates."

"You have to destroy that thing," Epona said. "Or take it from here to some distant world."

"It will not matter now" Bishop said. "The trail will bring her here. Even if the sword is destroyed or relocated."

"The Black Queen will learn the location of Earth and Tir na Nog," Titania said. "It was going to happen someday. How long before Leanne leads them here?"

"I have no idea, but if the Queen understands the bond, and I'm sure she does, they will begin following the trail soon. It will not be clear, and there will be missteps. Perhaps a month. Maybe two weeks. Longer if they delay."

"She won't delay," Morgan said. "I wouldn't."

"We allow the celebration to continue," the King announced to the small group. "In two days, after everyone is rested and recovered, we will begin planning to defend and to attack. Sionnach, you took the sword, you keep it. When the Dark Princess comes for it, I expect you to return it . . . forcefully."

"Aye, Sire," the Fae Warrior answered. "Though she should already be dead," he added.

Taking the blue blade from Bishop, he left the room.

"He had no call for that," Skerrit said to Cahal.

"He did," Cale replied. "I may or may not have killed her had I known about the bond."

"You would have left the sword behind," Titania said to the young man. "I saw in her the same thing you did, Dúnmharú. The spark once lit her mother's eyes, and still shines from our own Maerrighan. Those nearest the Reaper value life above all things. It burns within their souls. It burns within your soul, Cahal Kearney."

"I wonder which one," he replied aloud, but to no one specific. Did he value life as a human with ties to witchcraft, or as a Fae with no ties at all? Could a dark soul ever glow?

May 25, 2018

Appendix

Names Matter.

Cahal Kierney: Dark Descendant of Catharnagh

Sionnach: Fox / Catharnach: Soldier or Warrior.

Maerrighan: Night Mare Ruler.

Caileach Phisogach (The Black Queen): Veiled Sorceress.

Leanne Shee is derived from Leannán Sí, or Fairy-Lover.

Leathe Dimoni is from Liath, Irish for Grey, and Dimoni translates to Demon.

The Dark Princess' Royal Guard:

Donagh: Brown (haired) Warrior

Cornus: Horn

Caelan: Slender

Keara: Black

Nola: White Shoulder

Odhran: Little Pale Green One

And, of course,

Daegen: Black Hair

Other Terms You May Wish To Know:

Claidheamh: Sword. In this case, the title of the Seelie King's personal body guard.

Tir na Nog: Home world of the Fae. Literal translation is *Land of the Young,* or *Land of the Ever Young.*

Pandaemonium is the world of the UnSeelie. Roughly translated from Greek it means *All-Demon-Place,* though early interpretations said *Place of Little Spirit or Little Angel.*

Dúnmharú: Irish: Duine means *person.* Marbhadh means *killing.* Murderer is the most common translation, but the killing of another is not always criminal. It can also mean executioner, or assassin.

History Lesson: 1854 Broad Street cholera outbreak occurred in 1854 in the Soho district of London. six-hundred-sixteen people died during the outbreak. Dr. John Snow ended the outbreak with his discovery that contaminated water, not air, was the source of cholera.

This event is well worth studying as Dr. Snow's work is regarded as the founding of epidemiology.

I hope you enjoyed the latest adventures of Cahal Kearny and Annabeth Hughes. Nothing helps a writer reach more readers than someone who enjoys a story sharing their opinion with a review.

If you would take a moment more of your time, please go to your bookseller's website and leave your opinion for **THE FAVOR.** It is much appreciated.

Visit donfoxe.com for more on Dúnmharú and other literary works. On the CONTACT page, send me your email to receive my newsletter and the opportunity for a free book.

Don

www.ingramcontent.com/pod-product-compliance
Lightning Source LLC
Chambersburg PA
CBHW022106170626

46808CB00002B/628